Black Friday

James Kaine

THIS BOOK CONTAINS GRAPHIC
CONTENT

READER DISCRETION IS ADVISED.

PART I

MEET OUR CONTESTANTS

CHAPTER 1

L ogan Talbot's senses were fucked, overwhelmed by the cacophony of gunfire and explosions surrounding him, the deafening ringing, the result of the explosion that took out their helicopter, drowning out any sense of direction. As Logan wiped his face, his hands came away sticky with a mixture of sand, sweat, and blood. He could feel a sharp pain throbbing in his temple, a receipt from the impact. His taste was dominated by the coppery tinge of blood. It dripped down his cheek and his mouth from the large gash on the left side of his head as he lifted it off the ground. The metallic scent filled his nostrils, mingling with the dry earth and the burnt remains of the helicopter.

He wiped his face as he got to his feet, clearing his eyes so he could see enough to assess the situation. The squad's UH-60 Black Hawk helicopter lay before him, a twisted hunk of charred metal, its cockpit a mangled wreckage from the rocket strike. The air was thick with the stench of burning oil, the acrid smoke hanging heavily in the desert air.

Inside the cockpit, the devastated corpse of Jesse Griggs, the pilot for the ill-fated mission, burned in his seat. When the rocket hit, the explosion obliterated Jesse's cranium. The surrounding interior was painted with blood and chunks of skull and brain.

And it wasn't just Jesse. There were ten men on that helicopter, and most were not as lucky as Logan. The twisted, mangled remains of the Marines were strewn about the cabin among a gory mass of severed limbs and entrails. Bobby Davis was buckled in and folded in half, crushed as the metal frame bent upon impact. His eyes were wide and frozen in his final horrific moments. Danny Chang's face was vivisected by a piece of shrapnel that broke off and embedded itself just to the left of his nose. Chunks of gore sluiced down the metal, and his tongue dangled to one side, hanging by a small remnant of membrane. Ethan Redfield's head slumped unnaturally low, the shattered portion of his spine jutting out the back of his neck. Logan counted seven bodies in all. Two were unaccounted for.

Logan had been lucky, if there was such a thing as luck out there, that he was in the cabin's rear, the area that suffered the least of the impact. He had still gotten his bell rung pretty good, though. He was mostly numb at that moment, but if he survived, he would be feeling it for a long time.

Logan's hearing improved to where the gunfire sounded much closer. Tufts of sand kicked up in rapid succession as a barrage of bullets struck immediately to the left of his head. He barely rolled out of the way. He pushed up to his hands and knees and crawled the rest of the way around the rear of the devastated vehicle, pushing his back against it.

It was always going to be a high-risk mission. Logan's unit was tasked with taking down a Taliban stronghold. Intelligence had shown a large contingent of enemy fighters in a fortress in the southern part of the country.

Not only were forces gathering, they were also using the base to facilitate opium production. Bringing down that stronghold would have crippled the enemy's operation.

They were less than two miles from the target when the rocket took out their helicopter. It was January, so the temperature was only around seventy degrees, which would normally be a respite from the brutal summer conditions, but the intense heat from the burning chopper made Logan feel like it was the middle of July.

More bullets peppered the downed vehicle, clanging with each staccato impact.

Logan heard footsteps from the opposite side of the wreckage. He readied his rifle to put down whichever terrorist fuck thought it was a good idea to run up on him.

He didn't need to fire. Alex Vargas and Curtis Vaughn, two squad mates, joined him behind cover, narrowly ducking the latest salvo of machine gun fire. Despite the dire straits they were in, Logan was glad to see he wasn't the only survivor.

"Shit's fucked, LT!" Alex exclaimed.

LT was Logan's nickname for multiple reasons, most obviously because they were his initials. It also happened to be his rank—lieutenant. But the nickname actually pre-dated his time in the Marine Corps. Back when he played football in high school, in his hometown of Hamilton, New Jersey, his ferociousness at the linebacker position earned him the same nickname as New York Giants legend Lawrence Taylor.

Unfortunately for Logan, his high school accolades didn't result in a path to the NFL. He played as a walk-on at Rutgers, but mostly as a backup. It was at college, though, that he met Alex Vargas when they were assigned as roommates.

Alex was a skinny kid from North Brunswick. He wasn't as athletic as Logan, but he was smart, both in the books and on the streets. Despite their surface-level differences, the two hit it off. Logan showed Alex how to hit the weights, and by the end of their freshman year, he saw an impressive change in his physique. Alex, for his part, helped Logan through some of his tougher classes, allowing him to graduate on time and with a halfway decent GPA.

By the time they graduated, both men decided to join the Marine Corps, albeit for different reasons. Alex always had his eye set on joining the service, having come from a military family.

Logan was less clear on what life after college would look like once his professional football hopes were dashed. When Alex suggested they enlist together, it seemed like as good an idea as any.

Turns out, Logan "LT" Talbot was an even better Marine than he was a football player. Over multiple deployments to the Middle East, he earned numerous commendations and rose through the ranks. The brotherhood he found in the corps exceeded what he had during his time on the gridiron. Best of all, he had Alex, who had become like a brother to him, by his side.

That same brother was shouting into the radio for air support.

"FOB Phoenix, this is Spartan Five! Request immediate CAS at—" An explosion about ten feet away rocked the battered helicopter, breaking Alex's attempt at communication. "Fuck!" he shouted, before composing himself. Curtis leaned around the back end of the vehicle and laid down suppression fire, trying to give Alex time to finish the request. "Request immediate CAS at latitude 31.5830° N! Longitude 64.3600° E! Over!"

The garbled reply on the other end seemed to indicate the request was acknowledged, but there was no way to know for sure, because the continued gunfire made it hard to hear. Hopefully the UAVs were en route.

"We're sitting fucking ducks here!" Curtis yelled as he again leaned around to fire on the enemy. He got off half a dozen shots before Logan heard a whizzing sound followed by a splat. Curtis stopped firing and dropped his rifle at his side. His opposite hand clutched his throat.

"Curtis!" Logan shouted. "Are you okay?"

Curtis ducked back behind cover in time for his wobbly legs to fail him, sending him crashing down on his ass, his rifle dropping into the sand beside him. With his other hand free, he brought it up to join the first in covering his neck.

"Are you hit?" Alex asked frantically as he tried to get a look at him to assess.

Their squad mate didn't answer, not verbally at least. Curtis's eyes rolled back, and his grip on his throat loosened, his hands flopping to the ground as he lost consciousness.

As soon as his hands dropped, an arterial spray from the bullet wound in his neck splashed Logan's face. Alex rushed to cover the hole back up, but the flow was already slowing as the life drained out of their compatriot. He wasn't going to make it.

Logan bellowed and lunged around the side of the chopper, firing in the enemy's direction. "We gotta move!" he ordered. "Head for that dune!"

Alex joined him, and the Marines sprayed fire, sending the opposing fighters ducking for cover. If they could get to the other side of the dune, they could hold position until air support came in.

Logan's gun clicked empty, and he hurried to change the magazine as he ascended the dune, his body armor weighing him down. It made the climb slower than it could have been, but it was also the only thing protecting him from getting sliced up by the enemy. As he clicked the mag home, he heard another chaotic burst of machine gun fire, and his leg got taken out from under him. A searing burst of pain shot through his thigh, and he looked down as he continued to crawl, seeing a patch of red wetness blossom through the khaki camo of his pants.

"Mother fucker!" he shouted as he fired back toward the enemy. "I'm hit!"

Alex didn't need to be told. He already saw that and, a second later, grabbed him by the back of his armor, dragging him the rest of the way over the dune as they laid down more suppressing fire.

On the other side, they ducked as low as they could. With no targets in view, the opposition stopped firing. Logan knew they would approach, and if air support didn't get there soon, they would be done for.

Thankfully, within seconds, the UAVs flew overhead, and moments later, several explosions hit in the distance.

"The fucking cavalry's here!" Logan said as he turned toward Alex.

His heart skipped a beat when he saw his friend. Alex was slumped over in the sand. His face was gray, and his irises were drained of color. His skin looked withered and his body armor swallowed him. It looked as if he had lost a hundred pounds in only a few seconds. He was dead.

"Alex?" Logan asked, not believing his own eyes. "Alex!" he shouted, grabbing his friend, futilely trying to shake him awake. "ALEX!"

Logan snapped awake. It took him time to sort out his senses.

The first thing he saw was he was in a hospital room, but he didn't immediately trust his eyes. He felt dampness on his forehead, neck, and chest, his olive shirt soaked through to a darker shade. He also felt the uncomfortable rubbery faux leather of the hospital chair he sat in. The steady beep of monitors helped steady his focus, and the antiseptic smell permeating the room told him he was back to reality. His mouth felt dry, but he didn't taste blood or sand, and for that, he was thankful.

He leaned forward in his chair and ran his hand over his head. Even though he was going on three years since retiring from the military, he still kept his hair in the same tight fade he had when he served. Everything was coming back to him. The dream of that terrible day outside the Helmand Province was a frequent one, but Alex's fate was a more recent addition.

Logan looked at his friend, sleeping in the bed. The whir of the blood pressure cuff tightening temporarily joined the steady beep of the machines he was hooked to. Seeing him like that, it was no wonder Logan dreamed about him dying.

Unlike in his dream, Alex was still alive. He also looked mostly like he always did outside of being pale, but that was to be expected after just having surgery.

The procedure, a lobectomy, occurred yesterday. As the name suggested, they removed an entire lobe of his right lung to remove the tumor invading it. Turned out that exposure to burn pits with all kinds of hazardous waste permeating the air was a health hazard.

They found the tumor in mid-October, after Alex spent most of the summer and early fall fighting off multiple bouts of bronchitis and respiratory infections. His voice had taken on a hoarse, gravely affectation, which was odd since it always had a higher pitch to it. Logan and their other friends had always found it hilarious when he called for a pizza delivery and he would get very pissed off when the person on the other end referred to him as "ma'am."

The jokes stopped being funny when his cough started producing bloody sputum.

The weeks of scans and tests that followed revealed the existence of the tumor removed yesterday. The surgery went well, and Alex, aided by a generous dose of pain medication, was resting comfortably. But he still had a long road ahead of him. The next step was chemotherapy. Logan knew his friend was strong, and if anyone could beat this thing, it was him. The problem was all the treatment was going to be expensive, and VA benefits would only go so far.

Logan turned when he heard the door open behind him. He saw Alex's wife enter the room, holding two

Styrofoam Dunkin' cups. She looked tired, with dark bags under her eyes, and her demeanor was heavy with stress and worry. Still, she looked better than when she left, Logan having advised her to head home once the doctor confirmed the surgery was a success. She was freshly showered and wearing clean clothes. Her long blonde hair was damp and tied back in a ponytail.

Alex and Teri, having been together since freshman year of college, got married shortly before their first deployment. The couple clearly made up for any lost time in between Alex's stints overseas, because they had three kids—seven, four, and two—with a fourth on the way. Teri found out she was pregnant again three weeks before Alex's diagnosis. That many mouths to feed would only exacerbate their monetary worries.

Both Logan and Alex had been honorably discharged after being wounded during that fateful mission in 2021. Logan had been shot, just like in his dream. Alex had suffered a concussion—his third—and a spinal injury that, had it been any more severe, could have landed him in a wheelchair for the rest of his life.

Since returning home, Alex was working as an account rep at Brunswick Bank and Trust while studying online part time to achieve his master's degree in finance.

Teri worked part time as a hairdresser, fitting in clients out of her home when she could. With the staggering cost of daycare, working full time wasn't feasible.

Logan rubbed his eyes and offered Teri a smile. "You okay?" he asked. "Get any rest?"

She smirked. "Sure. I only had Miguel complaining his stomach hurt after eating too many chips, Gabriela asking when Daddy would be home, little Alex running around like a nut, and unnamed baby number four making me consistently nauseous. Very restful."

Logan stood and offered her his chair.

She walked around the bed and patted him on the arm. "But the kids need me. They don't understand why Daddy isn't home. Thank you so much for staying with Alex while I tended to them."

Logan nodded his acknowledgment and thanked her for the coffee. It was lukewarm, but that didn't faze him. He drank a whole hell of a lot worse while deployed.

"He's tough," Logan said, answering the unasked question. "He'll beat this thing."

Teri nodded and offered him a tight-lipped smile. She appreciated the sentiment, but a deep worry was written across her exhausted features.

"Why don't you go get some rest? I got it from here."

Logan and rest weren't exactly synonymous, but he wanted to give them their privacy when Alex woke up. He grabbed his jacket and draped it over his arm. His body temperature was still regulating after his sweat-inducing nightmare.

"If you need anything, call me. I'll be back before you know it."

She planted a light kiss on his cheek before taking her seat at her husband's bedside.

"Thanks, LT."

Logan took a step outside, and a blast of wind whipped his face, reminding him it was, in fact, November in New Jersey. It was the twenty-second. Thanksgiving was less than a week away, but it felt closer to Christmas with temperatures in the thirties. He slid his jacket on.

His car was a good distance away. This hospital always seemed to be packed. He wasn't surprised. Aside from the emergency room and inpatient offices, there were many physician offices located there as well, not to mention it was the go-to maternity center in Mercer County.

He was almost to his car when he heard a male voice with a British accent from his left.

"Excuse me, Lieutenant Talbot?"

Logan immediately went on guard mentally. Being addressed by not only his name, but his rank, in a public parking lot, was a red flag.

He turned in the voice's direction and saw a sharply dressed man approaching him. The stranger was tall, about six-foot-three. He had thick dark hair that was slicked back and wore an expensive-looking pinstripe suit with a matching silk tie and accompanying pocket square. Not that Logan was a fashion expert, but the guy carried himself like a person of wealth, or at least someone adjacent to it. It was in his gait and posture. His hands were visible out in front of him; the only thing he held was a plain white envelope, standard letter size, with LT. Talbot written on it.

Even though he didn't appear to be an immediate threat, Logan put his hand up to stop him. The man got the hint and halted in his tracks.

"Can I help you?" Logan asked cautiously.

"No, sir," the man replied congenially. "It's I who can

assist you. Or, more specifically, my employer can."

"Oh yeah? Who's that?"

"I represent Vortex."

Logan narrowed his eyes at the man, whose own expression remained even.

"That name supposed to mean something to me?"

"He's only the most-watched Internet personality in the world. But I can't say your lack of familiarity with him is particularly surprising. You don't strike me as someone who spends an abundance of time online."

He was right. Logan could probably count on one hand the number of times he watched a YouTube video. He never had social media, even back in college. Hell, he wouldn't even have an email address if he could avoid it.

"Yeah," he confirmed, "not a big internet guy."

"Yes well, Vortex's immense popularity is matched only by his wealth."

"What's that got to do with me?" Logan asked as the red flags mounted in his mind.

The man held out the envelope. "You'll find the answers in here."

Logan didn't accept it. "Yeah, I'm not in the habit of accepting sealed envelopes from strangers, with or without funny accents. No offense."

The sharp-dressed man smiled and casually reached into his jacket. Logan tensed, ready to act, but the man only pulled out a small Swiss Army knife, nothing Logan couldn't take from him if he made a move.

"None taken, Lieutenant Talbot," he said as he popped up the blade and used it to neatly slice the envelope open. "I understand your caution. After all, your hometown of Hamilton was the epicenter of the 2001 anthrax attacks, was it not?"

It was. And Logan wasn't the least bit comfortable with how much this stranger knew about him. Who the hell was he?

As the man removed a folded-up piece of paper, Logan watched intently as he ran his index finger along the surface before raising it and touching it to his tongue.

"Your caution is admirable, Lieutenant Talbot, but I assure you, this is only a piece of paper—one that can change your life." He held it toward Logan again. "Or perhaps you'll find its potential to help with your friend Corporal Vargas's predicament more compelling?"

"What the fuck did you just say?" Logan asked, taking a step toward the stranger, who knew way too much personal information for his taste.

The man raised his hands, and the paper, in a non-threatening gesture.

"I'm simply conveying the message from my employer. I have no compunction that you could give me a severe thrashing should you so choose, but let me remind you that I am unarmed, and we are in a medical facility parking lot with a number of security cameras."

He kept his hands raised but flicked his wrist to point the paper back toward Logan.

Logan felt his face flush with heat even as another gust of wind smacked into him. He *did* want to thrash him. His emotions were high, and there was no enemy toward which he could direct his anger. But he knew this wasn't the time or place.

He took another step forward and snatched the paper from the sharp-dressed man.

"Who are you?" he asked.

"I told you. I represent Vortex. The letter in your hands will apprise you of the details."

With that, he turned and walked away. Logan thought about following him and pressing him for more info, but he couldn't guarantee he wouldn't lose his cool and do something he would regret.

Logan watched the man step into an idling black Cadillac Escalade at the opposite end of the lot. It was only after it drove off that he opened the letter.

CHAPTER 2

"Liam!" Kasey Collins called to her eight-year-old son for the second time, her patience wearing thin.

Liam was sitting at the small table in their kitchen, completely dialed in on whatever he was watching on his tablet. He was in full-on zombie mode, an occurrence that was becoming too frequent for Kasey's liking. There were times she wished the well-worn device would crap out for good. Her son wouldn't be happy, but she could hang her hat on the very true fact that she couldn't afford a new one.

Still, that device was often her son's only outlet. For years, Kasey grew increasingly concerned about her son's lack of social interactions with kids and adults alike, fearing he may be on the autism spectrum. Finally, six months ago, she got an answer. A neurologist recommended by his pediatrician gave a dual diagnosis of generalized anxiety disorder and ADHD. It broke Kasey's heart to see her son struggle so much. She often found herself frustrated at her own inability to keep her cool with him at times, like when they were dangerously close to being late to school. Which, in turn, would make Kasey late for work. Again.

"Excuse me?" she asked pointedly as she leaned down

in front of him, forcing his sight line to her.

"What?" he asked, as if he was the one being inconvenienced rather than his mother.

"Go brush your teeth and get your shoes on," Kasey said as calmly as possible.

"One minute," Liam said as he turned his attention back to the device.

"No minutes," Kasey replied, less calm this time.

"Ugh!" Liam exclaimed as he got up from the table and stormed upstairs to brush his teeth as instructed.

Kasey sighed as she finished packing her son's lunch, stuffing it into his backpack and putting it by the door.

She listened to Liam finish up in the bathroom at the top of the stairs before his little footsteps moved down the hallway to his bedroom.

As she tied her dirty-blonde hair back in a ponytail, she thought, as she often did, that it wasn't supposed to be this hard.

And she certainly wasn't supposed to be doing it alone.

Liam was named after his father, Kasey's high-school sweetheart. They started dating when they were sixteen. Despite the usual cautions from well-meaning family and friends not to *get too invested* or *high-school relationships don't last*, Kasey and Liam were adamant they would be the exception.

And they were, for a time.

Liam proposed their senior year of college. They were married the following year. Liam got a job as a math teacher at the same high school where they met.

Kasey started working as a freelance photographer, her passion for as long as she could remember. She shot family portraits and birthday parties. She eventually wanted to shoot larger events like weddings and bar mitzvahs, but she knew she had to build a solid portfolio first.

She felt herself tearing up as she looked at the many pictures of her son that adorned the walls, both solo and just the two of them. Most of the photos were taken on her phone, her Nikon collecting dust at the top of her closet. Yes, the fact she had to put aside her dream of being a professional photographer in favor of the two menial jobs she worked to make ends meet made her sad. But what crushed her was the crucial element missing from the photos.

The love of her life, who never got to meet his son.

The day after Valentine's Day 2016 had been a Monday like any other. It was their first as a married couple, and Liam had gone all out. Flowers, chocolate-covered strawberries, and dinner at her favorite restaurant were followed by a night of passionate lovemaking. They had pulled the goalie, so to speak, as soon as they got married, but in the ten months since had not yet had any luck conceiving. Kasey remembered joking that if that V-Day session hadn't gotten her knocked up, she didn't know what it would take!

At the end of the following day, Liam was walking to his car after school. He was on the phone with Kasey, as he always was on his way home. They were talking about what they wanted to do for dinner when Liam's tone abruptly shifted.

He told Kasey to hold on. The next thing she heard was shouting, then a loud, booming sound followed by an ear-piercing scream before two more booms echoed over the line.

Kasey shouted her husband's name into the phone over and over but didn't get a reply. She jumped into her car and started the fifteen-minute drive to the high school, keeping the call active until it finally cut out. The last thing she heard before the call dropped was the wail of approaching sirens.

When she got to the school, the lot was jammed with bystanders cordoned off by police tape, preventing them from reaching the gaggle of first responders behind it. A Channel Six news van was parked to the side, under the flagpoles that flew both the school and American flags. A somber-looking female reporter wearing a navy-blue dress and heavy black pea coat held a microphone as she spoke into the camera. Kasey couldn't hear what she was saying, but the presence of police, EMTs, and the media were bleak indicators that something tragic occurred.

Kasey felt a surge of panic as she pushed through the throng of onlookers, making her way to the front, where Mary Breen, the school's principal—who had held that position since before Kasey and her husband were students—spotted her just in time to restrain her.

"Where's Liam?" she screamed repeatedly as the administrator struggled to hold her back.

"Kasey! You can't go back there!"

"Where's my fucking husband?" Kasey bellowed as she knocked Miss Breen aside, ducking under the tape. Before two uniformed offices halted her forward progress more effectively than the principal had, she saw three human-sized forms under blood-soaked sheets lying on the ground in the distance.

She dropped to her knees, and the world moved in slow motion. Everything around her went silent. She saw mouths moving and camera muzzles flashing, but she didn't hear the voices or the clicks of the shutters. She didn't hear Miss Breen say, "That's his wife." Nor did she hear the man in plain clothes with a badge and gun affixed to his belt trying to get her attention.

Kasey didn't need them to tell her what she already knew. One of those three bodies was her husband.

As Kasey later learned, Melissa Kennedy, captain of the cheerleading team, had been cheating on Sean Thompson, her football-player boyfriend. A lot. Sean found out when she unceremoniously dumped him on Valentine's Day. Her ex-boyfriend's response was to steal his father's shotgun and confront her.

When Liam saw the jilted teen approaching the girl, he tried to intervene and caught a shotgun blast to the face for his altruism. The scream that followed was Melissa, just before Sean blew a hole in her chest. He then placed the barrel in his mouth and pulled the trigger, turning his head into raw hamburger.

Kasey couldn't recall the events that followed in their entirety. Thinking back, the best way she could describe it was like trying to piece together the events of a drunken night out.

She recalled someone helping her off the ground and draping a blanket over her. Then she remembered sitting in the back of a police car. Next thing she knew, she was seated in a small room at the hospital, arguing with the detective who had tried to speak to her at the scene.

"I want to see him."

Her voice was barely above a whisper, but the detective heard her clearly.

"That's not advisable, Mrs. Collins."

"I don't care. I want to see my husband."

"Mrs. Collins, the damage to your husband was...considerable. That's not something you need to see."

Kasey slammed her fist on the arm of the chair. While much of that evening was a blur, she remembered the pain vividly. She also remembered welcoming it.

"I want to see my fucking husband!"

She didn't know how much time passed between her demand and when she stood in front of the body bag on the metal table in the sterile autopsy room. One detail that stuck out to her was the steady buzz emanating from the halogen lights bathing the room in a washed-out white glow.

The detective repeatedly tried to talk her out of viewing Liam's body, right up to the last moment before he gave the medical examiner the nod to unzip the bag.

As the nylon parted and her husband's head became exposed, at first, he looked like he was sleeping. His coloring was still normal, and his face looked mostly unblemished. But that was the right side. When Kasey saw the left, she vomited, the splat of her expulsion echoing as it hit the tile floor.

It wasn't just that the left side of his face was damaged; there was no left side of his face to speak of. It was just a concave crater of gore. There was no cranium on that side. No nose, either. Cracked remnants of teeth jutted from his gums, exposed due to him missing half his jaw. The shotgun blast turned her sweet husband into something akin to a prop in a horror movie.

She didn't remember anything else until she woke up in the emergency room. The detective informed her she fainted after she threw up, doing his best to avoid using an *I told you so* tone. She would have believed him even if she couldn't smell the foul chunks stuck in her matted hair.

The funeral was, of course, closed casket. The attendance was staggering. Beyond the large group of his many family members and friends, it seemed like the entire school showed up for a man who, in less than two short years, had become one of its most popular teachers.

Kasey was shocked at how well she kept her composure. Someone later told her the Thompsons tried to come in to pay their respects and offer their sincerest apologies, but someone spotted them and turned them away. That was good, because Kasey would have likely cursed them out for raising a little bitch who let some whore cuck him like that, costing her the only man she ever loved.

Deep down, she knew it wasn't their fault, and she probably would have regretted saying it to them, even if her sentiment about their son was something she stood by. But the rage and sadness at what was taken from her threatened to consume her, and she would have unleashed it on anyone who made the slightest of missteps toward her. Kasey Collins could very well have let that anger permeate her, turning her into a broken, angry person. And it almost did.

Until she found out she was pregnant the following month.

A flood of emotions washed over her as she sat on her bathroom floor, looking at the plus sign on the pregnancy test. Those feelings would be a rollercoaster over the next nine months, and on November fourteenth, Liam was born. Kasey remembered looking at the perfect little angel in her arms and thanking God she would always have this little miracle she created with her love before she lost him.

As Liam grew, Kasey did her best not to be overprotective or smothering. He was all she had. Five years after he was born, she had her first date since becoming a widow. It was okay, but nothing came of it. Dating was infrequent, sex even less so. Even almost nine years later, she could count on one hand the number of times she had been intimate with a man. She just didn't seem to have that desire anymore. Liam was the only man she needed in her life.

Therapy helped. It wasn't the cure-all she hoped it would be, but it helped to talk to someone. She saw an individual therapist for years and also took part in several grief-counseling groups. Seeing she wasn't alone in her trauma and loss didn't take the pain away, but knowing there were others in her situation eased it. Her sessions also helped her manage her instincts to over-parent her son, even though once his own issues with anxiety and ADHD surfaced, it became hard not to.

He was an incredibly smart, funny, and very creative little boy. Kasey could never understand why he couldn't bring himself to interact with the other kids at school. She would watch him walk up and stand ten, fifteen feet away from a group of his classmates running around, but not do anything other than look at them. She could see in his face he desperately wanted to be a part of the group, but for some unknown reason, he was just way too nervous to approach them.

Liam was seeing a cognitive-behavioral therapist of his own. It was helping, but it was a slow go. Kasey longed for the day she would pull up to school and see her child happily chatting it up with other students. Some days that seemed like a pipe dream. But she loved her son and saw so much of her late husband in him that she would keep trying to give him the life he descrvcd.

By the time they walked out of the house, Kasey resigned herself to the fact they were going to be late yet again. As they stepped into the cold and onto the wooden front porch, she felt the familiar pang of disgust at the peeling blue-gray paint. That was the defect that always stood out to her, even though it was only one of many throughout their modest home that direly needed renovations. The kitchen appliances were ancient, the furnace was well past its useful life, and the knowledge that the roof needed to be replaced turned her stomach.

Liam was droning on about his dissatisfaction at not being permitted to watch his tablet on the ride to school. Kasey had already been over it a million times that the ride was less than ten minutes, and if he needed the tablet for that limited amount of time, then he shouldn't have it at all. That was one morning where her internal pendulum was swinging toward less patience, and she was about two seconds from snapping at her son when something caught her eye.

A black Cadillac Escalade with tinted windows was parked directly in front of her house. The car was immaculately clean and waxed to a pristine shine. It definitely was not the type of car that would normally be parked in her lower middle-class neighborhood. She slowed her pace cautiously and drowned out Liam's droning as she regarded the vehicle.

When the door opened, she stopped in her tracks, putting her hand out to halt her son as well.

"Hey!" Liam said, annoyed.

"Shh!" she admonished the boy.

A tall, thin man with slicked-back hair and a fancy-looking suit stepped out. He wore a smile that did not, on the surface, appear threatening. In one hand, he held a plain white envelope. In the other was a rolled-up piece of black fabric. It looked like a shirt. Was this some kind of prank? Was Ashton Kutcher in the car behind those tinted windows? Was that even a thing anymore?

"Mrs. Collins," the man said in an English accent, "I'm glad I caught you before you left for work."

Kasey wasn't a detective, but she was observant. Two things in the man's sentence raised her suspicions. One was he called her *missus*. Kasey had not been married for almost nine years. In a vacuum, it wouldn't be so strange that a man would assume she was married, even if she no longer wore her ring on her finger. She had worn it on a necklace for the past six years. But that necklace was well covered under her blouse and jacket.

The other thing was when he said *caught you before*

25

you left for work. How did he know what time she left for work? Hell, the first question she should have asked was how did he know who she was and where she lived?

"Can I help you?" Kasey asked.

"No, Mrs. Collins, but I believe I can help you." He turned his attention to Liam, who was standing behind his mother, slightly to her right so he could see around her. "And what's your name, young sir?"

Kasey suspected the man already knew. Liam eyed him but didn't answer. Normally in this type of situation, she would urge her son to reply, but this was a stranger who showed up at their door. If anyone needed to show etiquette, it was him.

"What do you mean by *help me?*" she asked, brushing off his inquiry to her son.

He returned the favor by ignoring her and continuing to address Liam. "Heeding the classic mandate not to talk to strangers—you're a wise young man. You also look like a Vortex fan."

Liam lit up at the mention of Vortex. It didn't surprise Kasey. He loved watching Vortex's videos on YouTube. Kasey knew little about him other than he was very popular. She had vetted some of his videos before allowing her son to view them. She found them mostly benign, even if they were a little obnoxious. They consisted mostly of video game streams, reaction videos, and pranks. The pranks she didn't like, feeling they crossed the line from funny to mean. She also didn't like that he never showed his face. He always wore a mask with an LED display of a swirling vortex, hence the name.

Kasey reluctantly let Liam watch the other content with the caveat that if she caught him viewing the prank vids, she would take his tablet away for a month. She honestly didn't want him watching it at all, but with a child possessing Liam's challenges, she knew some level of compromise was necessary. She also knew a lot of the other kids at his school were fans of Vortex's content, and she didn't want to take away any in-roads he may have to social interaction.

The sharp-dressed man outstretched his arm to hand the shirt to Liam. Kasey intercepted it, snatching it before her son could. In the process, it unfurled, revealing the Vortex logo.

Liam excitedly grabbed it from his mother and held it up to his chest, assessing how it would fit. "Wow! This is my size! Thanks, mister!"

"You are most welcome, Master Liam."

Kasey had been momentarily disarmed by Liam's gleeful reaction to the shirt and his unprompted gratitude, but that went away as soon as the man addressed him by name. He did know it. In fact, he knew way too much about them. Was it some kind of data mining through the internet? It had to be.

"Come on, we have to go. We're already late," she said to her son, without taking her eyes off the sharp-dressed man.

As she started toward her car, the man extended his other hand and offered her the envelope.

"Of course, Mrs. Collins. I don't wish to delay you further. I simply want to deliver this envelope on behalf of my employer. You may find the contents have great potential to assist with your situation."

She hesitated but accepted it. "Who's your employer?"

The man chuckled. "Apologies. I didn't specify because I assumed you had drawn that conclusion. I represent Vortex."

He winked at Liam and offered Kasey a nod before returning to the Escalade without another word.

CHAPTER 3

"**F**uck me harder!"

The voice that shouted the explicit instruction belonged to Rachel Dubois of Newtown, Pennsylvania. The woman it emanated from, currently on all fours on the bed while getting railed from behind, was Scarlett Saint.

She was fully in character, playing up how much she was enjoying the sex for the phone camera capturing the action in 4K mounted on a tripod with a ring light in front of the bed. Anyone who watched the recording would think she was in ecstasy as she put on a masterful performance replete with dirty talk and multiple orgasms. What they would hopefully never know was it was all as fake as her pseudonym and bright red hair.

"Take it, you dirty fucking slut!" the man jackhammering away inside her increasingly aching vagina shouted. Rachel wanted to roll her eyes. For someone that had a reputation as one of the most popular male adult stars, his technique was trash and his sexy talk was even worse. But she played along.

"Yes, baby! Fuck my tight little pussy with that big dick!"

She wasn't lying about that last part. Kyle Mills, better known by his stage name, Rocco Reed—adult content creators apparently having a proclivity for alliteration—had an impressive body and a very large penis. It was what made him popular, along with another special talent. But his absolute lack of any consideration for his co-star made her wonder if the others he worked with had equally unpleasant experiences.

Thankfully, it was almost over. They had hit all the bases—blowjob, pussy eating, missionary, cowgirl, reverse cowgirl, and doggy style. There was only one thing left to do.

She looked straight into the camera while addressing her partner. "You ready to cum, baby? You ready to paint my pretty little face?"

Kyle picked up the pace and squeezed her hips hard, adding to her discomfort. Rachel's mouth went slack, and she hoped it would look like pleasure rather than pain for the audience.

"Fuck yeah!" the neanderthal said. "I'm gonna cum all over your fucking face."

Charming, she thought, hoping he didn't have a girlfriend. At least Scarlett was going to get paid for her trouble.

She pulled away from him, feeling relief as he withdrew from her swollen sex. She dropped to her knees, very aware of the camera's placement. The dolt followed and stood over her, but out of position. She grabbed his dick and yanked on it to guide him to the right spot to capture the grand finale.

I can't believe this dude's a professional, she thought as she spit on his organ and swallowed it as far as she could before gagging. She held it for a second before pulling her mouth off of it, using the strings of saliva to lube the shaft while she jerked it above her face. She had learned messier was better. The fans loved that shit.

It didn't take long for Kyle to grunt. She almost laughed, because it sounded like he was going to take a shit, but she stayed in character. The first rope of semen shot out and draped over her forehead and splattered into her fiery-red hair. The next plopped onto her outstretched tongue. She did her best not to retch as it dripped down to her chin. A few more spurts hit her in the neck and splattered her breasts before he finally finished ejaculating.

She hated every second, but this was one of the reasons she chose to work with Kyle. His aforementioned special talent was his ability to produce impressive money shots. She knew that would help bring her lots of views and, hopefully, a nice payday. No one watching would know how much she despised the whole act as she took his wilting member back in her mouth, portraying she was trying to milk every drop. When she was done, she smiled at the camera as she stood and approached it, standing right in front of the screen to show them her messy face as she winked and blew her future viewers a kiss before stopping the recording.

The minute the camera was off, Scarlett disappeared and Rachel Dubois was back. She ignored her co-star as she walked to the bathroom. She wanted to run, but her audience wasn't the only one she needed to put on a show for. Like it or not, Kyle was connected in the community, and if he started telling people she was a bitch to work with, she would be finished.

She stepped into the bathroom and felt like crying when she looked in the mirror. Her makeup, having been meticulously applied prior to the performance, was running down her cheeks. Kyle's semen was distributed over her face and chest and even matted her hair. She definitely couldn't leave the hotel like this. She desperately needed a shower but wanted to get rid of her co-star first.

Taking a deep breath and composing herself, Rachel slipped back into her porn persona.

"Damn," she said as she walked out of the bathroom with two towels, "your reputation is well-earned."

She tossed a towel to Kyle while she used the other to clean herself off, trying her damnedest not to reveal her revulsion. Kyle caught the towel and wiped his flaccid penis. Even in this state, it still looked enormous.

Rachel couldn't believe she had been able to accommodate it. It should look great in the final product. Still, it came at a cost. The ache between her legs told her she would need a break before doing another boy/girl scene. That was unfortunate, because those were her biggest money makers. She hoped to fit in another one before Thanksgiving next Thursday, thinking about doing a pilgrim theme, but fuck that. The one she just finished should bring in enough to hold her over.

"Thanks," Kyle said as he cleaned himself off and gathered his clothes. "You're pretty fucking awesome too. I hope I wasn't too rough with you."

That surprised her. Was he really that oblivious? Either way, she wasn't going to burn a bridge. "All good. You're a lot to handle, though, but I'm sure you know that."

Kyle smiled. It was almost sheepish. Compliments were like kryptonite to a guy like him, and she watched him melt in real time. A big dick didn't always translate to big-dick energy.

"Thanks," he said again. "I'd love to work with you again soon."

Doubt it.

"I'd love that," she lied. "I'll shoot you a text when the vid goes live."

"Sweet!" he said as he put his jacket on and slipped into his sneakers. "Can't wait to watch it back!"

I'll bet.

Rachel removed her phone from the tripod and flipped through before tapping the screen a few times. A second later, Kyle's phone buzzed. "Just sent you your cash," she said with a wink, staying in character even though she hated having to pay her co-stars up front.

He glanced at his screen and smiled. "Got it. Thanks!" He pocketed the phone and walked toward her. He leaned in to kiss her goodbye but pulled back at the last minute, most likely remembering what he did only a few minutes prior. Instead, he leaned in for an awkward side hug.

Rachel was polite and waved as he rounded the corner and left the hotel room. Once he was gone, she couldn't get into the shower fast enough.

After she washed the external remnants of the sex off, taking great care to thoroughly wash her chemically-colored hair with her special shampoo multiple times, she turned the water temperature as hot as she could take it. She stood under the spray for several minutes before slumping down to the shower floor. Once there, she drew her knees into her chest and rested her head on top of them.

Moments later, the tears flowed and mingled with the water as it swirled down the drain.

An hour later, Rachel was showered and dressed in a simple outfit comprised of jeans, a sweatshirt, and a winter jacket. Her bright-red hair was tied in a bun and concealed under a ski cap. It was probably overkill. She had fans, but she wasn't *that* famous. Sure, she got recognized fairly regularly, but it was rare that anyone approached her given her line of work. It did amuse her when she would catch a guy giving her a knowing glance only to quickly look away before his wife or girlfriend noticed.

Who's she?

Oh, I watch her get fucked in the ass on the internet because you won't let me do that to you.

She checked out of the hotel on the television, cringing at the nearly $600 folio. But what was she going to do? Rachel fully subscribed to the philosophy of fake it 'til you make it. Fucking in a Red Roof Inn might bring in some subscribers, but she wanted a higher class of viewer. Maybe such a thing didn't exist in the world of pornography, but she at least hoped to entice men with deeper pockets.

As she stepped into the elevator, she focused on the dull ache between her legs. She also thought about how expensive producing that scene was. Aside from the $600 for the hotel, she had to pay Kyle $1,500. That was up front, before she even made a dime from posting it on her fan site. There was the $200 on new lingerie, because she would be damned if she was gonna wear the same outfit twice on camera. After that, when you factored in gas, cell phone service, and internet provider, the meager profit she was going to earn would hardly make the discomfort she was feeling in her vagina worth it.

She had recently been thinking none of this was worth it, but she was in too deep. And it had cost her too much—not just money, either.

Rachel always wanted to be a star. Starting around five-years-old, she was always singing, dancing, and performing for anyone who would listen. Throughout her school years, she took classes in dance, piano, and acting. She tried out for every school play, snagging lead roles in *Anything Goes* her junior year and *Music Man* her senior.

Unfortunately, her experience and grades at her small Pennsylvania high school weren't enough to get her accepted to schools like Juilliard or NYU. Undeterred in her assertion that Broadway was in her future, she applied to Seton Hall University. It wasn't a school known for its theater program, but it was in South Orange, New Jersey, just a short train ride to New York City, which was crucial when the auditions inevitably started rolling in.

Only, they never did. She tried so hard, buying subscriptions to *Actors Access* and *Backstage*, scouring them daily for new postings and submitting them only to be met with crickets. In return, her friends tried to urge her to start small, maybe community theater, but she didn't want to hear it. Broadway or bust, baby!

She eventually graduated with a liberal arts degree, and

even though the bright lights hadn't found her yet, *she* found something worthwhile—her boyfriend, Darren.

They met in a gym class they both took the second semester of senior year. It was a bullshit elective they each took for different reasons. Darren opted for it to get a break from his more arduous finance classes. Rachel took it because her education was never her priority and she was just trying to graduate on time.

The two hit it off right away, their differences complementing each other. The physical chemistry was intense, sure. They first slept together within a week of meeting. But beyond that, Rachel loved how driven and career-focused he was, while Darren admired how she wasn't afraid to throw caution to the wind and chase her dreams. It was like they each had that element the other was missing.

After graduation, they moved in together to an apartment in Short Hills, close to Seton Hall. It was an upper-class area, but Darren landed an excellent job at a New York City accounting firm right out of college, and they found a place they could afford if they were responsible with their money.

Two years after graduation, Darren proposed. Rachel was over the moon. His career trajectory seemingly had no ceiling, and the financial security he would provide could allow her to keep chasing her dreams.

It was around that time Rachel pivoted away from theater and toward film. She got a few auditions, and even a callback, but no roles. Just as she was about to give up, her luck changed. A chance encounter with Mike Platt, a former classmate of hers, put her on a trajectory she thought would result in her dreams coming true.

Mike had gotten a job with a casting agency, and he

had a few roles he thought she would be a good fit for. He proposed a dinner meeting to discuss. Darren called bullshit, but Rachel was insistent, showing him his card and LinkedIn profile to confirm.

Darren was still uncomfortable, but she insisted he had nothing to worry about. Turns out, he did.

Even though Rachel promised not to meet with Mike, when Darren went away for the weekend for a training seminar, she took a chance. In her mind, she would meet up with Mike, and by the time Darren got back, she would be signed with his agency. He would probably be mad, but he would get over it when he found out it was strictly business.

That may have been Rachel's intention, but during a dinner full of lofty promises, they drank several bottles of wine. Rachel always had an issue with alcohol. She wasn't a drunk by any means, but she rarely realized she was in danger of consuming too much until she already had. So when Mike suggested they continue the conversation at his place, any semblance of good judgment was out the window.

Two hours later, she was crying in a cab back to the apartment she shared with her fiancé. Yes, she had been drinking. Yes, it was stupid. But she knew damn well what she was doing and what she was putting on the line when she had sex with him. It was only when they finished that she even considered the possibility Mike may be full of shit. But the damage was done.

Darren was sitting on the couch waiting for her when she got home. He had gotten home a day early and wanted to surprise her. A wilting bouquet sat on the coffee table in front of him. His eyes carried a hollow look as he looked at her wrinkled dress and smeared eyeshadow.

He knew what happened; she didn't even try to hide it. She broke down and sobbed, dropping to her knees in front of him and throwing her arms around his waist, begging for forgiveness. He pushed her off and grabbed his suitcase, still packed and sitting by the front door, and walked out.

That was the last time she saw him.

He didn't return her calls or texts, blocking her after the first couple hours of her attempting to contact him. An email two days later told her the lease, which was in his name only, was up in two months. He would let her stay there until then on the condition that she leave for one day so he could pick up his things. She thought about agreeing to those terms but staying, even though she would have told him she was away, so they could talk. But she ultimately thought better of it. The night she got home and confirmed all of his belongings were gone was the night she realized it was truly over.

Trying to do the right thing, she had left her engagement ring in an envelope on the coffee table, but he didn't take it with him. Somehow, that made her feel worse.

Worse, but not as bad as when she found out Mike was full of shit. He had only been an intern at the company for a summer. He just didn't update his LinkedIn. The scumbag even had phony business cards made up, and Rachel had fallen for it hook, line, and sinker. The dude was just a scammer trying to get a piece of ass, and Rachel was naïve enough to fall for it, the stars in her eyes blinding her common sense. And it cost her everything.

She pawned the ring for probably a third of its actual value. It was still quite a bit, but she knew she couldn't afford to stay in Short Hills without a job. Even if she could get something, it likely still wouldn't be enough. Despite everything, she couldn't force herself to go back to Pennsylvania. Maybe South Orange would be an option, but that town carried too many memories that had become painful for her. Ultimately, she moved a little farther south, to Old Bridge.

She tried different jobs over the next months—retail, waitress, receptionist. Nothing stuck, and the money she was making wasn't enough to maintain even her meager studio apartment. One night, while a little tipsy and scouring the internet for side hustles, she came across a video about selling feet pictures for cash. Intrigued, she found a site and set up an account. To her surprise, people started buying her pics. Even more surprising were some of the special requests she received. Guys would message her asking her to do things like step on a cake or a plate of spaghetti or to pour chocolate syrup on her toes. Those requests made her even more money.

It wasn't long before she started showing a little more of her body, along with her feet. It started with shots that included her ass or crotch covered in short shorts. Then it was in her panties. Before long, she was showing everything. That led to more money, but it still wasn't enough. She started looking into the online-model fan sites. Again she signed up and started showing her full body—first in bikinis and lingerie, then topless, then fully nude. When that still didn't put her where she wanted to be financially, she moved into the realm of hardcore and had been there ever since.

As she stepped out of the elevator, walked across the lobby, and went out the front doors to the valet stand, she felt that nagging regret of where her life was and where it could have been. She should have been married for a couple of years, maybe even with a kid, or at least one on the way. At that moment, the concept of ever having a family seemed like a bigger pipe dream than her previous dreams of being on Broadway. Who the hell was going to want a girl who did the things she did on camera?

She handed the valet the ticket and felt numb, wanting nothing more than to get home and crash into her bed. She would upload the video tomorrow.

While she waited, her thoughts were interrupted by a man's voice with an English accent.

"Excuse me, Ms. Dubois?"

She turned and saw a tall, thin man with slicked-back hair wearing a fancy-looking suit standing next to her.

"Who are you?" she asked. At first she thought he was the rare fan who both recognized her *and* had the balls to approach her, but there was something odd. He addressed her by her real name, not her stage name. She was very careful about keeping the two separate, so it couldn't be that.

He held out a plain white envelope. "I've been instructed to deliver this to you."

"What is it?" she asked.

"An opportunity. A chance to do something with your life beyond fornicating on camera."

What the fuck? she thought. He knew who she was? Both on screen and off?

"What did you just say to me?" she asked, anger burning inside of her. "Who the fuck do you think you are?"

"I'm simply a man tasked by my employer to deliver a message to you."

"And who the fuck is your employer?"

"I represent Vortex. I trust you're familiar with him?"

She had heard of him. He was some type of online streamer. Rumor was he had been with some of the top girls in her industry, but they were tight-lipped about it. She guessed he had them sign some pretty iron-clad NDAs. Beyond that, she knew little. His content and hers didn't exactly align. Was that what was going on? He wanted to add another model to his conquests?

"I'm not an escort, dude."

"I didn't imply that you were, Ms. Dubois. Or do you prefer I address you as Ms. Saint? I apologize, as I am not familiar with the etiquette here."

"Call me whatever you want. Not interested."

Wasn't she, though? What if this Vortex guy wanted to hire her to be his girlfriend for the night, or even a weekend? It would probably pay well, and she wouldn't even have to film it. A one-night stand cost her the chance at marriage and kids and led to her fucking random men on camera. Why the fuck would she have any compunction about taking cash to have sex with some internet dork?

She turned back to the sharp-dressed man and saw he was still looking at her, hand outstretched with the envelope. She took it.

Once she did, the man signaled to his left, and a black Cadillac Escalade pulled up in front of them. It must not have been the valet driving, because no one got out. The man got in the back and nodded to her.

"Good day, Ms. Dubois."

CHAPTER 4

"Stay with me, Manny," Steve Bell instructed before delivering another punch to the drug dealer's jaw. It stung his fist, but Steve was sure it didn't hurt him nearly as badly as it did Manny. The blow sent a spurt of blood out of the scumbag's jaw and across the brick wall behind him.

"Where's your stash, Manny?" Steve asked, grabbing him by his collar and slamming him into the wall. He looked dazed as the back of his head smacked into the brick. He probably had a concussion.

"Fuck you, pendejo!" Manny said defiantly.

Fuck me? Steve thought. The lowlifes had flooded into his old neighborhood in Trenton, forming gangs and running drugs and guns, yet somehow Steve was the asshole? He thought not. As payback for the insult, he drove his knuckles into Manny's gut, sending him doubling over, while bloody saliva drooled from his mouth. He held Manny there for a few moments, letting him think about his words before pulling him back up and slapping him across the face.

"Don't you know you can't speak to an officer of the law like that, you little piece of shit?"

Steve was indeed a cop. A detective, in fact. But, despite his position, he had always seen the law as more of a guideline, one he was following less and less as he got older. At fifty-one-years old, he was fucking tired. His body was breaking down from years of alcohol and unclean living. Abs had given way to a paunch, and the hair around his temples was graying. His cardio wasn't great, but he could still pack a punch from his early days as a boxer. Like they said in *Rocky Balboa*, a fighter's punch was the last thing to go. He was four years away from retirement and a pension that wouldn't do nearly enough to cover his debts. To make matters worse, the money he owed wasn't to American Express. It was to some really bad guys, much worse than Manny and his little pissant gang buddies.

Steve hadn't seen another option in life other than becoming a cop. His entire family had been cops, and his dad had really pushed him to follow in his footsteps. It wasn't like he really had any other ambitions in life. Plus, the badge seemed to come with a level of power and status he figured he could use to his advantage. And that he did.

From the time he was in uniform, it wasn't uncommon for Steve to use his influence to get what he wanted. If he pulled over a pretty, young thing for going ten miles over the speed limit, a blowjob would prevent her from getting a ticket that would no doubt cause Daddy to take away her convertible. When he busted some dumbass kid dealing pot in the park, he would take his stash and run him off with a mess in his pants. The kid would be unlikely to get back in the game, and Steve could turn around and get some cash for the drugs. He saw it as a net positive.

But as Steve progressed in his career, so did his vices.

Booze was always a thing. He liked his bourbon, and

not the cheap shit, either. Fortunately, there were plenty of bars that would give him a discount if he looked the other way if they served the occasional minor or allowed local prostitutes to peddle their wares, for which they would deliver a cut to the establishment. They also let him sample the merchandise himself whenever he felt like reminding those worthless whores the only reason they could operate was because of him.

Aside from all that, Steve's major addiction was gambling. Poker, craps, slots—he did it all, and usually at a not-insignificant loss. He wondered more than once why he couldn't stop doing something he clearly wasn't very good at. Still, he found himself in Atlantic City or hopping over to Parx in Pennsylvania just about every weekend. He justified it by telling himself he didn't have a family to worry about, so who the fuck cared what he did with his money?

That logic would have been sound, but he, like every other type of addict, didn't know when to say when. He was always running at a deficit, and his kitchen table was more often than not stacked with piles of past-due notices. He could throw his weight around as a city police detective in local settings, but with banks and utility companies, not to mention those rat fucks at the Internal Revenue Service, Steve didn't have any influence to exercise.

His situation got so bad that, for the past five years, he was on the payroll of Carmine Capelli, one of the most notorious mafia dons in the state of New Jersey. Sometimes it seemed like every cop in the state was either working for him or trying to put him behind bars. It became like an ecosystem, where the honest cops and the corrupt ones were balancing each other in a kind of cold war. If the depths of Carmine's influence were ever made public, it would result in a massive overhaul of almost every department in Jersey.

Steve never lied to himself that he was a boy scout. He knew he lived his life in the gray, probably leaning more toward the dark side than the light, but he never planned on getting involved with the mob. But he also didn't intend to drop thirty grand, his entire life savings, on a poker game. He knew damn well it was a mob game when he sat down, but his ego told him they wouldn't fuck with a police detective. His ego turned out to be a fucking idiot, because when he couldn't pay, he caught a hell of a beating for his trouble. Fortunately, they kept away from his face, making it a little easier to hide it from his colleagues, explaining his ginger movements as the result of a fall down the stairs. They assumed he was a drunk, but that was better than knowing he was into the mob for well over five figures.

Ever since then, he had been working off that debt, but because of the outrageous vig, not only had he not made a dent in the principal, but the interest had ballooned his total owed to over fifty grand at last accounting. Steve didn't have any illusions that was by design. Carmine was a fucking multi-millionaire, and Steve's debt wouldn't make an impact one way or another to his bottom line. His value was his badge, and as long as he could keep the heat off Carmine's operations in Trenton, that debt would never be repaid.

"I'm going to ask you one more time, cocksucker," he said to Manny, who looked like he was close to losing consciousness. "Where is your motherfucking stash?"

Manny was a mid-level dealer, but Steve knew he had good shit. Recently, Steve had taken to rolling gangbangers where he could, snatching their drugs and cash and selling them to the bigger operations. He did this because he could get away with it when it came to the smaller fish. He wouldn't have to worry about retaliation from the more violent gangsters who had no compunctions about taking the fight to the police. If he was careful, he could also stay under Carmine's radar and build up enough cash to disappear. Sure, Carmine had a long reach, but he wasn't the fucking CIA. If Steve could disappear to Barbados or Costa Rica or somewhere like that, he doubted the mob would come looking for him.

Steve felt his rage bubbling over at Manny's stubborn refusal to give up the goods. He wanted nothing more than to bash his head into a bloody pulp right there in the alleyway. It wouldn't be the first time he killed one of the lowlifes, so he knew he would get away with it. Maybe Manny's mama would shed a tear or two, but no one else would. Steve reached into his holster and pulled his Glock 17, thrusting it under Manny's chin and pushing his head back as the barrel indented the underside of his jaw.

"Listen here, fuckface," he said through gritted teeth. "I'm going to count to three, and then you're going to tell me where. The fuck. Your fucking. Stash is."

"I ain't tellin' you shit, cabrón." His voice was pained, but his tone was determined.

"One," Steve said, pushing the barrel up farther, eliciting a grunt of pain from Manny but not the information he wanted. "Two..."

Manny hocked a bloody loogie at Steve, spattering his left cheek.

"Mother fucker!" he shouted as he wiped it away with his free hand, his rage turning his vision red as he fought with every fiber of his being not to pull the trigger. It wasn't supposed to have gotten this far. He really thought he would smack Manny around a bit and get what he wanted, but Steve had severely underestimated the kid's stubbornness. He was barely twenty; most of the younger thugs would fold almost immediately. But not the stupid fuck in front of him.

Steve wasn't even sure if he was going to pull the trigger on three. On the one hand, he couldn't just let the asshole call his bluff. He couldn't risk the meager reputation of fear he had built among the local gangs. On the other, he didn't really want to kill the kid. Even beyond the mess he would have to clean up, Manny didn't really deserve to die for Steve's fuckups.

As he was about to say three, still not sure what that would result in, a loud bang pierced the night. The right side of Manny's head exploded, sending a geyser of blood splashing across Steve's face.

He didn't immediately let go of the drug dealer's corpse, but the dead weight started dragging the body down. Manny's head lolled back, and Steve could see the entry wound where his eye used to be, the chewed-up brain matter visible through streaked gore in the empty socket.

When he got his bearings after a few seconds, Steve let the body drop into the muddy puddles at the foot of the building. He turned and pointed his gun in the direction of the kill shot, immediately finding himself blinded by a pair of headlights at the exit of the narrow alleyway. He did his best to keep his eyes open as he addressed the unseen assailant or assailants.

"Trenton PD!" he shouted, doing his best to seem authoritative. "I haven't seen you, so it'd be in all our interests for you to walk away! No one gives a shit that you just blew away a scumbag drug dealer! Least of all me!"

Whoever was driving the car killed the headlights, and Steve could see the car clearly. It was a black Mercedes S-Class, and he knew who it belonged to before he even saw him walking around the car, the black tiger-stripe Desert Eagle he used to obliterate Manny's face still smoking.

Dominic Capelli. Carmine's son.

Dom was only twenty-five and a real hothead. It wasn't uncommon for him to go rogue, and he had made more than a few messes his father needed to clean up over the years. Anyone else would have gotten two in the back of the head, but these guineas were big on family, so it didn't surprise Steve the amount of leeway Carmine gave the petulant little shit.

He was flanked by another of his father's guys, Jimmy DeVito, a big bastard that had done stretches everywhere from Trenton State to Rahway. Jimmy didn't have a weapon out. He was casually lighting a cigarette, but Steve knew he could do plenty of damage with just his bare hands. He had seen the case files.

"But I do give a shit, Steve," Dom said as he approached, while the beleaguered detective lowered his gun but didn't holster it. "You see, you're not as smart as you think you are."

"I don't know what you're talking about, Dom. I'm working on a case."

"Don't insult my intelligence, Steve."

That ain't too hard, Steve thought, but seeing as how he let himself get compromised, he had little room to hurl insults. "What are you talking about, Dom?"

JAMES KAINE

"Put that gun away," Dom said, his voice turning to stone. "We want this to be a friendly chat."

"What about yours?" Steve asked as he slowly curled his finger around the trigger.

Dom narrowed his eyes as he regarded the detective. For a long second, Steve thought he would have to try to shoot his way out of the alley, but Dom couldn't hold his mean mug anymore and cracked a big smile. He laughed as he shoved the gun into the rear waistband of his jeans before patting Steve on the back and putting his arm around him like old pals at the bar.

"You're way too uptight, you know that, Steve?" He pointed to him but looked toward Jimmy. "Didn't I say that to you the other day, Jimmy? You could shove a lump of coal up Steve Bell's ass and get a diamond!"

"You did say that, Dom," Jimmy replied in an uninterested tone as he blew a plume of smoke into the air.

"See?" Dom asked as he removed his arm and stepped in front of Steve, straightening out his jacket. "You gotta stop being so uptight."

With that, he punched Steve in the stomach, sucking all the air out of him. With his cardio being subpar, he didn't have that much to spare. His legs buckled and gave out as he put all his energy into getting his breath back. He dropped to his knees next to Manny's corpse. His lungs burned and he hacked violently, the last one bringing up some undigested chunks of the gas station hot dog he ate for dinner.

Dom crouched down next to him and put his fingers under Steve's chin, lifting it so the detective could look at him through his watery eyes.

"As I was saying, you've gotta stop being so uptight,

50

because your desperation is making you do stupid things. Like thinking you can earn without paying up to my dad."

"I...don't know what...you're talk–"

Dom slapped him across the face. It was hard enough to get the point across, but not so forceful as to disorient Steve further.

"I guess you didn't hear me say not to insult my intelligence."

Steve spit out another bloody, phlegmy chunk of undigested frankfurter and adjusted himself to a seated position against the wall.

"What do you want me to do?"

Dom stood up and looked at the beaten cop. "We have so many eyes and ears across the state, Steve. I thought you knew that. I really thought you knew better than to think that we wouldn't know that you were rolling these street-level shitheads. We also know why. You're trying to run, Steve."

"I'm not."

Dom kicked him in the face, sending his head splashing into the puddle of blood pouring from Manny's ruined cranium. He immediately tried to push himself up, and Dom rewarded him with another kick to the ribs for his effort, sending him crashing back down, resulting in a mouthful of the bloody alley water. When Steve pushed himself back into a sitting posture, Dom let him.

"Please don't lie to me again, Steve. It makes me upset."

"He gets very upset when people are dishonest," Jimmy confirmed.

"Jimmy knows. Honesty is the best policy. That's why I'm going to be honest with you." He crouched to Steve's eye level. "You see, you've never been a great investment for us. Sure, you had your uses, but you've never had anything resembling finesse or skill. To be honest, I don't see anything you bring to the table that would compensate for your character flaws."

"Dom—"

"Shut the fuck up, Steve!" Dom snapped before evening his tone again. "Here's the deal. Your services to our organization are no longer required. That means you have to pay back our investment in you. By my count, that means you owe us $52k and change. So let's call it $53 even. We don't round down in our business."

"Dom, you know I ain't got that kinda money."

"That's a you problem, my friend," Dom said, standing up. "You have until the day after Thanksgiving to pay up or..." He trailed off but nodded to Manny's body. "Nah, I don't gotta say it out loud. I think you know."

"Dom, come on, man."

"Friday, Steve. No more extensions."

With that, Dom left the detective sitting in the alley, next to the dead drug dealer.

After Steve cleaned himself up and dumped his clothes—too much of Manny's DNA was on them and he had no interest in his wardrobe being evidence in a murder investigation—he found himself sitting at the bar at Garton's Pub, the Maker's Mark doing little to ease the aching in his ribs, which were no doubt severely bruised at minimum. He downed the remnants of his second glass and signaled the bartender to pour him another.

The Irish pub was a popular hangout among the cops in the city. It was far enough away from gang territory that they didn't have to worry about their drinking being interrupted by gunshots or other disturbances. The space was dimly lit and adorned with dark, polished wood furnishings, exuding a sense of antiquity. The walls were lined with weathered photographs, yellowed newspaper clippings, and vintage Gaelic signs, proudly displaying the heritage. It was one of the few bars in the city that eschewed the non-smoking laws, and the air was thick with the stench of tobacco mingled with the aroma of aged whiskey.

It was Monday and close to eleven p.m., so thankfully, the place was mainly empty save for a few of the regulars who practically haunted the joint.

"You may want to slow your pace, Steve," said the bartender, a man in his sixties with a generous amount of salt-and-pepper stubble that matched his shoulder-length hair.

"And you may want to mind your own fucking business, Ray," Steve snipped back.

Ray gave him a disapproving look but filled his glass anyway, not offering another word as he turned his attention to other patrons, no doubt feeling it best to stay away from the irritable policeman.

Steve brought the glass to his lips, feeling a twinge of pain in his battered ribs.

He didn't even bother to turn when the door opened, but he was dimly aware of Ray sounding a little thrown off when he greeted whoever it was that walked in.

"Eh...grab a seat wherever, pal. I'll be with you in a sec."

He became aware, however, when he heard the barstool next to him scrape along the weathered tile floor.

What the fuck?

"Hey buddy, all these empty stools and this is the one you pick?" Steve asked as he turned to see a tall, sharp-dressed man with slicked-back hair and a pretty damn expensive-looking suit. He spoke in a British accent.

"Apologies for my forwardness, but it is you I'm here to see, Detective Bell."

For fuck's sake, haven't I had enough for one night?

"Who are you?"

"I represent Vortex."

"What the fuck is that supposed to mean to me?"

Ray interrupted by asking the man what he could get for him.

"Seltzer water, please," the man said.

Ray gave him a puzzled look. Not a lot of patrons waltzed into that place and ordered anything other than beer or whiskey. Regardless, he placed a glass in front of the guy and used the soda gun to fill it.

The British guy took a dainty sip before placing it back on the waterlogged cardboard coaster. Then he reached into his jacket and pulled out a plain white envelope, placing it on the bar and pushing it in Steve's direction.

"What the hell is this?"

"That is something with the potential to solve your, let's say, dilemma."

"What do you know about my *dilemma?*" he said, trying and failing to mock the man's accent with the last word.

"I know that were I to owe a substantial sum of money to Carmine Capelli, I'd have quite a bit of trouble sleeping at night."

Steve felt like he had been kicked in the stomach again. How the fuck did this guy know about his issues with the Capelli family?

"What the fuck did you say?" Steve asked, lowering his voice to a whisper.

"No judgment here, Detective. Simply an option to solve your problem."

"Listen here, you limey fuck. I don't trust people who come up to me and offer to magically solve my problems."

"No magic, Detective. And please, do try to maintain some decorum. You appear to be getting worked up. I don't think you want to draw any attention to yourself by getting cross with me."

Steve took the envelope from the bar and turned it in his hands, looking for some indication as to what may be inside.

"Who or what is Vortex?"

"I assume you know how to use Google, Detective. That will tell you what you need to know. The contents of the envelope will explain the rest."

With that, the man stood and placed a crisp hundred-dollar bill next to the glass from which he had only taken the single sip. He signaled toward Ray.

"Barkeep, Detective Bell's tab is on me. Please keep the change for yourself." He turned back to Steve. "Have a good evening, Detective."

CHAPTER 5

Eléna Mendoza stepped out of the registrar's office of Princeton University in total shock. She squeezed every facial muscle, trying to hold back her tears. The ache in her left knee, still healing from surgery six weeks ago, felt that much more painful in light of the news she just received, the crushing weight of the knowledge that her financial aid was denied.

Eléna was a sophomore at Princeton and the first in her family to go to college. Her paternal grandparents were first-generation immigrants from Ecuador who had settled in a small town in Texas. They were hard workers but couldn't afford to send her father to college. Her mother's family, who had immigrated from Honduras, was in a similar situation. Now, with three children of their own, Eléna's parents were committed to working hard for their family to afford them the opportunities they missed out on.

While she had the grades to get into an Ivy League school, her family, no matter how hard they worked, just didn't have that kind of money. Fortunately, Eléna was an exceptional soccer player and received multiple scholarship offers, including a full ride to Princeton. She still remembered her euphoria at opening the letter, scarcely able to believe it was real life and not some kind of prank.

What was not so fortunate for Eléna, however, was the ACL tear she suffered in the second game her freshman year. She vividly remembered hearing the pop, followed by her knee buckling and failing to hold her weight as she crumpled to the ground. Her teammates helped carry her off the field, and she knew before she even reached the locker room that her season was over.

Ever determined, Eléna started rehabbing as soon as she could post-surgery. She maintained strong discipline in getting up at six a.m. every morning and going to the field to do strengthening and coordination exercises. Rain or shine, hot or cold, she was there every single day. Getting back on the field for next season was her top priority. Not because she had any aspirations of playing beyond college. Sure, it would be nice to make the U.S. National Team, but there were lots of girls as good as, or better than, her. Plus, this early injury issue dimmed her chances even further.

For Eléna, it was critical to get back on the field to maintain her scholarship so she could finish her major in political science. She wasn't going to win a gold medal, but she was going to change the world for the better. Growing up poor gave her a perspective on the struggles of her community. She was still in high school when she started noticing the empty platitudes of elected officials, where they would promise funding for education or the arts or community development while seeking election only to fail to deliver on any of those promises once they were in office. A degree from a university as prestigious as Princeton would give her a significant jump start on that career.

Eléna didn't even make it to the first game of her

sophomore year. She stepped on the practice field sporting a protective brace on her right knee, pain-free and ready to work. Halfway through the third practice, she felt that same pop, only this time on her left. She fell to the ground again and hid her face in her hands, not wanting her teammates to see her tears.

The second surgery was also a success, but Eléna knew the bad news was coming. She got it three weeks ago. Two ACL tears in two years with only one game played wasn't enough to keep her on the team. She was cut, and as a result, her scholarship was revoked. As vividly as she remembered the award letter, she also would never forget the hollow emptiness she felt as she read the revocation notice. It was written in a sympathetic tone, but that meant little when the words themselves punched a hole in her heart.

She called home in tears, and her parents assured her they would do everything they could to keep her enrolled. But Princeton was one of the most expensive universities in the country. Still, they were true to their word, assessing their savings, exploring cashing in their meager investments, and looking at their options for student loans.

Ultimately, it was all a moot point. The Mendoza family could liquidate all of their assets and still not have enough to carry her through graduation. Not only that, they had two other children with ambitions of their own. José was in his junior year of high school and a computer whiz. He had his eye on MIT, and even though it looked like a scholarship was in his future, it wasn't a guarantee. Luís was only in eighth grade and hadn't decided what he wanted to do in life yet, but mortgaging the future of two other children for one would not be fair.

That left financial aid as Eléna's hope. A missed checkbox on page four dashed those hopes. The provost, Mr. Laymon, delivered the news in the same sympathetic tone as the letter revoking her scholarship, but as her father was fond of saying, the only place the word sympathy meant anything was in the dictionary.

She pled for a chance to correct the forms, but Mr. Laymon told her it was too late. The deadline had passed. After informing her she was out of options barring a miracle windfall, she went numb. She could finish out the semester but wouldn't be able to return after Christmas break.

As she exited the office and made her way back to her dorm, the sky was gray and overcast above the ivy-draped buildings. The architecture of the campus, with its intricate construction, had always inspired awe but barely registered as she passed the buildings that day. The drizzle of rain that started prior to her meeting was falling at a steady pace, the drops creating a rhythmic patter as they hit the ground. It had rained on and off throughout the day, so the air was redolent with the scents of wet grass and earth. It was cold, colder than usual for this time of year in New Jersey, or so she had been told. Definitely colder than Texas. The wind cut through Eléna's clothes, the elements particularly harsh on her, specifically her still-rehabbing knee. She shook it off as she shuffled like a zombie toward the dorm that would no longer be her home after next month. The fading daylight felt like it was also the twilight of her hopes and dreams.

About halfway there, she felt weak in the knees. Her surgically-repaired ligaments had been deemed fine to walk on, so it was more likely the emotional weight of an uncertain future that crushed her.

She made her way to a nearby bench. The bronze plaque displaying the name of a donor, in this case someone named J. Ketchum, had taken on a teal hue over the years. She plopped onto it, not giving a damn how wet or cold the wood was, especially since her clothes were already soaked.

The dam finally broke, and she buried her head in her hands as she sobbed. Thankfully, the campus was largely a ghost town, with most of the students having returned home for Thanksgiving break. She didn't really care if anyone saw her. Once she went back home, she would never see any of these people again.

In a daze, there was nothing in the immediacy that could compel Eléna off that bench. It barely registered to her when the raindrops stopped hitting her head. But she did notice the shadow that fell over her, followed by the patter of the downpour shifting to a plop, as if landing on a barrier.

She looked up and saw a tall man standing over her. He was thin, with slicked-back hair, and wore a suit. She had no idea if it was expensive or not, but it looked nice. The man held an umbrella out far enough to shield both of them from the rain as he smiled. It was a friendly gesture, but something about it gave Eléna the ick.

"You'll catch your death of cold, sitting out here in the rain," the sharp-dressed man said in an English accent.

"Listen, man. I'm having a bad day, and I'm really not in the mood for...whatever this is."

"That is evident, Ms. Mendoza. I imagine it's quite rare to find a young woman with such a morose demeanor sitting in the rain whilst having a *good* day."

"How do you know my name?" Eléna asked, her guard

up while simultaneously cursing herself for confirming he correctly identified her.

The man avoided the question and handed her a plain white envelope. "I've been instructed to deliver this to you on behalf of my employer."

She took the envelope, again only considering it may have been inadvisable to do so after the fact. Her heightened emotional state was clouding her better judgment.

"What's this? Who's your employer?"

"I represent Vortex," the man said matter-of-factly.

"The YouTube guy?" she asked.

"That's a bit reductive, but yes."

She was tangentially familiar with the content creator, mostly because of her brothers. Luís, in particular, was a big fan of his video game streams. Eléna mostly zoned out when he tried to tell her about them.

"Am I on camera?"

The man looked both ways and behind him, as if trying to figure that out for himself. "It would appear not, Ms. Mendoza."

"So, what's this about?"

"You'll find the contents of that envelope will explain everything. What I will tell you is that it may very well hold the solution to continuing your education."

That got her attention. While she wasn't overly familiar with Vortex, she had seen plenty videos of influencers surprising people in dire financial straits with cash prizes. She wasn't naïve enough to believe the motives of people who relied on clicks on views for a living were rooted in altruism, but if it helped her stay enrolled at Princeton, did it matter?

She accepted the envelope and stuffed it in her jacket,

her best option for keeping it dry.

"You're still a way from your dorm, Ms. Mendoza," the man said. His depth of knowledge about her again sent a chill through her body. "Would you like me to escort you with my umbrella to shield you from the weather?"

Eléna surveyed her surroundings. The campus remained largely empty, with that particular area completely devoid of students or faculty. She again chastised herself for not carrying the small vial of pepper spray her father had given her before sending her off to college. "Just because it's an expensive school doesn't mean you shouldn't be careful," Daddy had said.

"No, thank you," Eléna told the man, hoping she was firm enough to drive the point home but polite enough not to raise his ire. Sure, he presented as some kind of proper British gentleman, but she didn't know anything other than he worked for an internet celebrity and somehow knew way more about her than she could possibly be comfortable with.

"Understandable," the man said as he took a step back. "Discretion is the better part of valor."

With his umbrella no longer shielding her, she again felt the raindrops pelt her hair. She waited until he turned the corner before getting up from the bench.

She quickly followed, still holding the envelope in her jacket. When she rounded the corner, he had already descended the steps and was walking toward the opulent non-denominational chapel that stood as one of the university's most majestic structures, its ornate stained-glass windows casting colorful reflections in the puddles. She watched as he stepped into an idling black Cadillac Escalade. He didn't spare a glance in her direction as the SUV drove off.

CHAPTER 6

"**D**inner in five, boys!" Teri called from the kitchen.

"Sounds good," Alex said, his voice low, trying not to strain for fear of eliciting a coughing fit, straining his damaged lungs.

Logan looked at his friend sitting in the easy chair in the living room of their modest two-story home in North Brunswick. Teri had always done her best to maintain a clean house, but having three kids with another on the way and a husband sick with lung cancer and limited in his ability to help put a damper on those efforts. She apologized profusely about the state of the house when Logan showed up for Thanksgiving dinner, but Logan reassured her the house looked great. Compared to some hovels he had to make camp in while on deployment, that wasn't an exaggeration.

Alex cleared his throat, and Logan was afraid for a moment he would indeed start coughing. It would be painful, and it would pass, but his chief concern was the kids seeing their dad hack up blood. Alex Jr. was busying himself playing through the battle he and Logan set up with his container of army-men figures. Miguel was engrossed in a game of *Roblox* on his tablet. Gabriela had her nose in a *Goosebumps* book. Logan offered to help Teri in the kitchen, but she politely declined, nodding toward Alex to let LT know his efforts were better directed toward spending time with his friend.

The second of three NFL games was on the television, and the Giants were surprisingly holding their own with the Dallas Cowboys, the score tied at ten going into the second quarter. Alex was covered in a custom blanket Teri got him with a collage of pictures of their family. She mentioned she would have to order a new one when baby number four arrived.

Logan knew from his time helping out that the majority of Alex's medication was kept in the upstairs bathroom, but he had an inhaler and a bottle of painkillers on the table next to him. Underneath, a medium-sized air purifier hummed as it rotated back and forth, doing its best to keep the air as clean as possible for his ailing lungs.

"Chow time!" Teri called. The kids halted their various activities and made their way to the table. Logan thought that was a credit to Alex and Teri that their children would stop what they were doing when their parents called.

Alex flipped off the television and started to get up but struggled, both because of his weakened lungs and the soreness of the surgery he was still recovering from. Logan gave him a few beats before he went over and offered his hand. Alex frowned but accepted the help.

"I fucking hate this shit, LT," Alex whispered, needing to vent but not wanting his family to hear. "All the shit we been through, and a fucking tumor's got me reeling."

"And you'll kick its fucking ass just like you did those insurgents," Logan emphasized, keeping his voice down as well. He gently patted his friend's arm. "You got this, big dog."

He let go of Alex but kept an eye as his brother-in-arms slowly made his way to the head of the well-loved wooden dining table with mismatched chairs. He made it without impediment and took his seat, with Teri on his right and Gabriela on his left. Logan took the seat at the opposite end, flanked by Alex Jr. and Miguel.

Teri had prepared a modest but no less mouth-watering spread for their holiday dinner. Each place setting had been arranged neatly with the children's help. A construction-paper outline of their hands modified into the shape of a turkey had each diner's name written across the palm. The plates were plain white, and the sterling-silver cutlery set Teri inherited from her mother rested atop neatly folded napkins.

A medium-sized roasted turkey, a perfect golden brown, was the centerpiece of the meal. Other serving dishes circled the platter, containing a variety of sides—homemade stuffing with herbs, celery, and chunks of bread baked to a delicious crisp, creamy mashed potatoes, cranberry sauce, green beans, and soft, warm dinner rolls. Alex Jr. found the turkey-shaped butter particularly amusing.

It was a truly impressive meal under normal circumstances, but Teri had gone above and beyond to make this holiday as special as it could be given the current status of things.

"Gabriela, sweetie, why don't you say the blessing?" Alex said.

"Why does Gabi get to do it?" Miguel asked.

"I'm giving that privilege to the oldest this year. Gabi has been a big help to Mom. Not saying you haven't, but she's done an especially good job." Miguel didn't protest further but looked disappointed nonetheless. "Your time will come, son."

The family held out their arms, and each grabbed the hand of the person next to them on either side, forming a circle.

Logan followed along even though it wasn't a tradition he was comfortable with. He couldn't explain why; he just didn't like it. But he was a guest in their house, and he wasn't about to be rude. He closed his eyes, along with the Vargas family, as Gabriela started the blessing.

"Bless us, oh Lord, and these thy gifts which we are about to receive from your bounty, through Christ our Lord, amen."

Logan opened his eyes and loosened his grip, but he stopped as she continued.

"Thank you for this food. Thank you for our friends and family. And thank you for helping my daddy get better after his surgery. Thank you for not taking him from us."

That last line was too much for Alex as he was the one who broke the chain and lowered his head to hands, heaving sobs wracking his body.

"Daddy?" Miguel asked, concerned as the other kids looked on.

Teri got up from her seat and embraced her husband. She said nothing. She just held him and let him get the emotion out, sparing an apologetic glance toward their dinner guest.

"Daddy, why you cry?" Alex Jr. asked.

Alex composed himself enough to choke out an apology. "I'm sorry, bud," he said through a sniffle. "I'm just so blessed to be home with you guys."

The kids all got up as if sharing one mind and joined their parents in an embrace.

As Logan watched the family express their love for one another, he actually got angry—angry at the universe for letting Alex survive such a fucked-up situation as war only to hit him with a deadly disease when he thought he was through the worst of it. At that moment, they were undergoing a new battle. Logan would give anything to cure the cancer, but he couldn't. He could be there for them to lend support like he had been, but that wasn't enough, in his mind.

He thought about the piece of paper in his pocket and understood there was one thing he could do that would truly help them.

When he arrived home after his encounter with the British man in the hospital parking lot, he removed the letter and read it.

Dear Lieutenant Talbot:

You are cordially invited to Vortex's

BLACK FRIDAY BATTLE

What:
A contest where one contestant can win up to FIVE MILLION DOLLAR
in cold, hard cash!

Where:
Oatbridge Mall in Lawrenceville, NJ

When:
The stroke of midnight on November 29th, 2024

Do YOU have what it takes to win??

This contest is INVITATION ONLY and HIGHLY CONFIDENTIAL.
Disclosing any information about this event will put the
contestant at risk of disqualification and forfeiture of any pri
money.

See you on BLACK FRIDAY!

Logan was a pragmatist. It was hard not to be given the things he had seen over the years. He wasn't given to flights of fancy or long shots like playing the lottery. He always stood by the saying wish in one hand, shit in the other, and see which one gets filled first. But looking at his friend and his loving family, he was helpless in the face of an enemy they couldn't shoot or bomb. Logan didn't have a lot of options to help them.

Except one.

Kasey didn't have much of an appetite.

She watched Liam happily eat the mac and cheese she brought with her to her parents' Thanksgiving dinner. As usual, her mother, Debra, went over the top, with no detail spared. Except, of course, consideration for Liam's self-imposed dietary restrictions. Kasey tried exhaustively to improve her son's diet, but to no avail. She would cut up a rotisserie chicken and veggies, putting it on a plate in front of him with the threat he wouldn't get anything else, but his endurance was damn near legendary. He would, more often than not, wear her down until she made him some type of pasta or toss some dino nuggets in the microwave.

Her parents, her mother especially, thought the whole thing was ridiculous, so she made no type of accommodation when they came over for dinner. Kasey always found it ironic how she said she longed for family time but did so little to actually make Kasey and her son feel welcome. She actually thought her mother was offended he wouldn't eat her cooking, no matter how many times she emphasized he barely ate *anyone's* cooking.

Kasey learned long ago to take matters into her own hands, bringing one of Liam's limited meal preferences whenever she came over. Her mother didn't like it, but she at least didn't protest. Most of the time. That night she had made a snide comment about all the work she had put into the meal, but if her grandson wanted to stick with a boxed dinner, then it was his loss.

That wasn't to say her mother wasn't correct about the spread she prepared. The large mahogany dining room table at her parents' elegant Robbinsville home was full of mouth-watering dishes, highlighted by a magnificent roast turkey, its skin perfectly browned and garnished with fresh herbs. It was surrounded by stuffing, creamy mashed potatoes, green beans with toasted almonds, and homemade cranberry sauce. None of that canned bullshit, Debra promised. In the kitchen sat an assortment of pies—apple, pumpkin, and lemon meringue.

Her father, William, sat, along with his wife, at the head of the table, the space large enough to accommodate two. On the right hand sat her sister, Keri, and her husband, Ethan. They had three children: Evan, Brayden, and Harley. On their left sat her maternal grandparents, Vernon and Ada, miraculously still kicking in their early nineties. Kasey and Liam were at the opposite end of the table, which a lot of times felt like exile, but she would never dare voice that because she already knew her mother would brush her off and her father didn't have the spine to stand up to his wife.

"Can I have some mac and cheese?" Brayden, her sister's middle child, asked.

"Of course, sweetie!" Kasey said as she reached for the bowl.

"No thank you, Kasey," Keri said with a smattering of disdain. "He can eat what's in front of him."

Brayden looked disappointed but didn't protest.

Kasey hoped her face wasn't turning as red as it felt.

70

Her sister always had a way of irritating her. Not so much by what she said but, often, by what she *didn't* say. She had politely, in the loosest sense of the term, declined, but what she was really saying was that her children would do what they were told and she wouldn't give in. Unlike her sister.

She turned to Liam and rubbed his back. "How's your food, kiddo?" He didn't answer as he stuffed another spoonful in his mouth. "Liam?" she asked again, with no reply.

"Liam!" Debra snapped, finally getting his attention.

"What?" he asked. Kasey knew his tone wasn't intended to be rude, but it came out that way, regardless.

"It's rude not to answer when someone is speaking to you, young man."

"Sorry," he said as he slumped in his chair, defeated. It broke her heart to see him like that. Kasey knew his very real diagnosed conditions, no matter what excuses her mother made, were the reason for his behavior, and trying to force him out of it was not a helpful strategy. She tried to perk him back up.

"Are you excited about putting up our Christmas tree tomorrow?"

That was always a tradition for Kasey and Liam. Christmas was their favorite holiday, and it was their tradition to put up the tree and lights the day after Thanksgiving every year so they could get the maximum enjoyment out of the season. Something about the way her modest home looked when decorated for the holidays filled Kasey with joy.

That was getting increasingly more difficult. For the past three years, she had been scheduled for the night shift at Schow's Department Store, because it was always all hands on deck for Black Friday. At least her day job as a receptionist at Skipp and Spector, a local law firm, was a lot more lenient, a fact she was grateful for, especially with her troubles getting to work on time.

But, despite how tired she was when she rolled in the next morning, they always took the time to put up the decorations before she took a nap. They would put *A Christmas Story*, Liam's favorite holiday movie, on repeat as thcy worked, and they would cap it off with a glass of eggnog—Kasey's enhanced with a splash of Southern Comfort. It was one of the rare times Liam was fully engaged. She didn't care how tired she was; she wasn't going to miss that.

"Yeah!" Liam beamed. "I'm already working on my list!"

"List?" Evan asked.

"Yeah! For Santa! I didn't get a gaming PC for my birthday, but I *know* Santa is going to bring me one this year!"

"You still believe in Santa?" Evan asked derisively.

Liam looked at Kasey with devastated bewilderment, like his world had just been shattered. Kasey's vision turned an angry shade of red as she shot her nephew a death glare.

"Of course he does. But it doesn't surprise me you don't." She turned back to her son. "Evan doesn't believe because Santa only brings presents to good boys and girls, not spoiled little shits like your cousin."

"Excuuuse me?" Keri said as she yanked her napkin off of her lap and whipped it onto the plate in front of her. "Just who the hell do you think you are, speaking to my son like that?"

"Me?" Kasey said, surveying the table in a futile attempt to seek backup. "How could you be okay with him saying something like that to my child?"

"Maybe if you didn't coddle him so much, he wouldn't have these issues."

"And maybe if your husband could keep it in his pants, you wouldn't need to go fuck yourself!"

A collective gasp rang out from the table. This blowup had been a long time coming. Sure, it was a low blow to bring up her brother-in-law's infidelity, but everyone knew about it, including Keri. They just didn't talk about it. Kasey hit her breaking point with her family, acting like they were so above her because they had money and status while she struggled. Every one of them had a skeleton in their closet, yet they acted like Kasey was the odd one.

"C'mon, Liam," she said as she stood from the table and took her son's hand. "Let's go get a pizza."

A few hours later, when Liam was tucked into bed, Kasey gave some last-minute instructions to Jennifer, her neighbor's daughter, who was an immense help in babysitting when she had to work the night shift, and headed out.

As she stepped onto the porch and felt the chill in the air, she reflected on how the evening ended. The most telling thing was no one in her family tried to contact her. She wanted to cry. Not because she had any great love for her family—hell, her life would be infinitely less stressful without them—but that didn't mean she was happy with her situation. She pulled the piece of paper out of her purse and reread the invitation to Vortex's Black Friday contest. The top prize was five million dollars.

Kasey had resigned herself to the fact she wasn't able to take part because of her job. She couldn't sacrifice steady income for a miniscule chance to win a life-changing sum of money. But she also knew it would take something drastic to turn her life around. What if she actually won? Someone had to, right? She took a deep breath and made the call.

Rachel sat alone at her kitchen table, a half-empty container of house lo mein in front of her. She was wearing her favorite pair of fuzzy pajamas, a far cry from the type of outfit her fans were used to seeing her in.

Comfortable as they were, it always pained her to wear them. She had had them since college, and they used to be a fun joke between her and her ex-fiancé. Whenever she came out of the bedroom wearing them, Darren would give her a look of mock disappointment and say, "Looks like I'm not getting any tonight!" They would share a laugh, because that was rarely the case. Often, she would wear lingerie underneath, and before long, the fuzzy pjs were tossed aside.

When she wore them since that time, she felt the pain of their breakup all over again. But she welcomed it. She fucking deserved it.

She scooped up some more lo mein and chewed it. It was fine. Not exactly a bountiful Thanksgiving feast, but what was the point if she didn't have anyone to spend it with?

Her phone rested on the table next to the takeout container. The screen was black, and she had silenced her notifications. She felt down enough without getting a message from some lonely pervert asking to buy her used panties.

Rachel picked it up and stared at it for a few moments, contemplating if she was really going to go through with what she intended to do.

As her heartbeat quickened and her palms moistened, she scrolled through her contacts. She found the one she wanted under D and held her thumb over it for close to a minute before she finally found the courage to call her father.

She watched the screen light up with a picture of her with her father from her high school graduation under the text that read Daddy. The fresh-faced girl in the green cap and gown was only vaguely familiar to the woman sitting at the table wishing desperately for her father to pick up and tell her to come home, that it would all be okay.

Rachel was nervous on the first ring, then hopeful on the second. On the third, the call cut out. Did he send her to voicemail?

Maybe the phone just cut out.

On the second attempt, it barely rang once before it went to voicemail, the intentionality no longer in doubt.

She squeezed her eyes shut, but not in time to stem the tears. Fighting to keep from a full-on breakdown, she placed her phone face down on the table, holding no hope her parents would have a change of heart and call her back.

They were furious when they found out the reasons behind her broken engagement. Her father, in particular, grew frustrated with her lack of ambition. Following your dreams was one thing, but she had gone too long with too little to show for it. When her flights of fancy cost her the love of her life—whom they adored—it became even more foolish in their minds.

But she was their daughter and they loved her, so they did their best to support her after the breakup. However, when a family member sent them the link to her fan site, that was the final straw. A brief but blistering email from her father made it clear they no longer wanted a relationship with her. That was almost three years ago. She hoped they would cool off and reconsider having cut her out of their lives, but that hadn't happened. Tonight confirmed it never would.

She stepped away from the table and moved to her bedroom. On the dresser was the folded-up piece of paper from the envelope the British guy gave her the other day.

Rachel dried her eyes and reread the information on Vortex's Black Friday contest. Five million dollars could buy her a new life. She could still start over.

In that moment, Rachel decided to stop lamenting the past and start looking toward the future.

Steve sat on his usual bar stool at Garton's Pub.

Being it was Thanksgiving, only the truly downtrodden frequented the joint that night. Steve supposed that was him. His folks were long dead, his two ex-wives wanted nothing to do with him, and he was still sore from the beating he had taken from Dom.

As he sipped from the glass of Maker's, he felt it burn as it slid down his throat. The sip became a gulp, and by the time he put the glass back on the bar, it was empty. He was about to shout to Ray for another when the bartender emerged from the kitchen, holding a plate.

He placed it in front of Steve, who picked up the turkey on rye with Swiss cheese, lettuce, and tomato, and took a bite. With his free hand, he pointed to the glass for Ray to pour him another.

It wasn't a gourmet Thanksgiving feast, but the joint had shockingly good food for a dive bar. Ray poured Steve another glass of bourbon, along with one for himself. He raised it to the detective for a toast.

"Happy Thanksgiving, Steve," he said.

"Same to you, bud."

The detective downed his drink and brought the sandwich up to his mouth for another bite. As he did, his phone buzzed, and he instantly lost his appetite. He didn't want to look, but he did anyway.

D: Tick Tock

He put the phone back and forced himself to take another bite. If he didn't have Dom's money by tomorrow, he was well and truly fucked. His only salvation was the piece of paper in his pocket.

"Eléna, wait up!"

Despite the plea, Eléna kept walking toward the Uber waiting for her just outside the university gates. Her teammate and roommate, Whitney Gamble, was running to catch up to her. Given Eléna was still recovering from her surgery and Whitney was in top shape, she knew she couldn't outrun her.

Eléna had hoped she could slip out of the dorm unnoticed. The handful of the team that stayed behind for break organized a Friendsgiving. Eléna smiled through it, doing her best not to let the emotion of knowing her college career was over put a damper on the evening. Kelsie and Nicole did a great job recreating a traditional Thanksgiving dinner in their dorm. Even though the food was ordered from a local restaurant and not cooked fresh, all the elements from the turkey to the stuffing to the mashed potatoes were there.

She excused herself when she finished the meal, giving the excuse she forgot something in her room, but Whitney, a criminal justice major, was a goddamn human lie detector. Her roommate knew she was full of shit the second she opened her mouth.

Eléna was quick to grab her coat and the invitation to the game at Oatbridge Mall. It was only a couple miles from the university, but she didn't have a car and the bus schedule was sporadic, so she ordered the rideshare. She was barely ten steps out of the dorm when Whitney burst out the door behind her.

"Where are you going?" her roommate asked as she caught up and started matching Eléna's slower, but steady, pace.

"I have to take care of something."

"What?"

"I can't tell you."

Whitney grabbed her arm, gently but firmly, to stop her.

"What can't you tell me?"

Eléna wrenched her arm away and snapped, "It's none of your business!"

She started walking again, but Whitney followed, undeterred.

"Lanie, you're acting weird."

She and Whitney were both from the South, Eléna from Texas and Whitney from Tennessee, although the latter's accent was much more pronounced. She was the only one who called her Lanie, and she found it as endearing as it was annoying.

"Says the girl chasing after me across campus."

"Ugh!" Whitney groaned. "You are so frustrating, you know that? I thought we didn't keep secrets, but you've been off for the past few weeks."

"No, I haven't."

Whitney grabbed her arm again, and this time, Eléna didn't try to pull it free.

"You got cut."

It wasn't a question.

"You know?"

"Sweetie, of course I know. It doesn't take a detective to figure out that they weren't keeping you on after your second ACL tear, no matter how fucking unfair that is."

"Yeah," Eléna nodded. "It's really fucking unfair."

She started to cry, and Whitney pulled her in for a hug.

"Hey, hey. It's okay."

"No, it fucking isn't!" Eléna shouted into her friend's shoulder. She let out the emotion that had built up since the registrar's office for a few moments before adding softly, "They're kicking me out, Whit."

Whitney pulled back but kept her hands on Eléna's shoulders. She was three inches taller, so she crouched slightly to look into her friend's red, watery eyes.

"What?"

"I lost my scholarship. And my financial aid got fucked up, so I'm done."

"Oh my god! I'm so sorry!" Her sympathy twisted into irritation when a sudden realization hit her. "So you were going to just leave without saying goodbye?"

"No! It's not like that. I...just have somewhere to be."

"Where?"

"I can't tell you."

"Oh, hell no! You ain't running off and doing something crazy."

"It's not, it's just...confidential."

"You ain't in D.C. yet. You don't get to sneak off on Thanksgiving night and pull the confidentiality card."

Eléna was growing frustrated. It was worse when her phone buzzed and she saw the impatient message from her Uber driver requesting an ETA.

"I really have to go," she said as she started walking again, Whitney following right along with her.

"Fine. Let's go then."

"What?"

"If you go, I go."

CHAPTER 7

L ogan pulled his pickup truck into the parking lot of Oatbridge Mall. As the structure came into view, abandoned the past eighteen months, the latest casualty of the e-commerce juggernaut, a wave of nostalgia washed over him.

This was the mall he frequented growing up. When he was a child, he would often accompany his mother on shopping trips with the hope he would get to spend some time in the play area with its plastic animal sculptures and coin-operated rides. Or maybe he would be given some quarters to play *Street Fighter 2* or *Teenage Mutant Ninja Turtles* at the Space Port Arcade. If it was a *really* special day, they would see a movie at the four-screen theater downstairs, after which he would be allowed to pick up something small at Kay-Bee Toys.

As he got older, the arcade and movie theater were replaced by more stores, but he still spent many a night roaming the mall with his friends. The food court was the most popular hangout, but they also snickered at the crude t-shirts or sneaking a peek at the sex toys in the back of Spencer's Gifts. But those days were long gone for Logan, a distant memory, along with the innocence and optimism stolen from him by war. He honestly never expected to set foot in this building again, even long before it closed.

As he followed the posted signs that guided him to the main entrance, he questioned if he was really going to do this.

Five million dollars would cover Alex's medical expenses and then some, but he had no idea what the contest entailed. He knew fuck all about internet culture. Could he even be competitive?

Logan stepped out of the car. The nondescript hoodie he opted for instead of his military surplus jacket provided little protection from the cold. As he approached the entrance, he saw a few people walk in ahead of him. When he was about twenty yards away, he noticed the sharp-dressed man from the hospital parking lot standing in the entryway, the sliding doors held in the open position.

Just like the other day, Logan's guard went up, but for a different reason. The man was flanked on either side by two large, bulky men. He had clocked the Brit at about six-three, but these guys were both several inches taller and significantly more muscular.

Everything about them, from their suits to their stances, screamed private military company.

Logan slowed as he got closer, but the sharp-dressed man lit up when he saw him.

"Lieutenant Talbot! I'm so pleased you decided to participate in our little contest, although it would be disingenuous of me to say I expected you to show up."

"Yeah," Logan said, addressing the man but sizing up the goons. "What's with the muscle?"

"Come now, Lieutenant, surely you don't think we would run a contest offering a multi-million-dollar cash prize without a robust security detail?"

He had a point. Still, these guys weren't retired cops babysitting a bank. These were the type of guys you hired to protect VIPs who didn't qualify for Secret Service protection. Or to make those that did disappear.

Logan didn't take his eyes off the security as the man ushered him inside.

Ten minutes after Logan Talbot walked into the mall, Kasey pulled into the spot adjacent to where he had parked his truck.

She was shaking as she turned off her car. Her call to Mr. Gonzalez, her supervisor at Schow's, had not gone well. Kasey couldn't totally blame him. An employee calling out a few hours before the biggest shopping day of the year was an issue, especially when sales like that were crucial to keeping the brick-and-mortars in business.

So yes, she understood Mr. Gonzalez's position. That didn't make it any easier when he told her she was fired. His exact words were, "If I can't count on you when I need you the most, I can't count on you at all."

That cut her deeply. Not because working retail was some illustrious career, but work was hard to find. Her receptionist job alone wasn't enough to support her and her son, yet because of one emotional decision, it was their only source of income at that moment. She had let her mom and sister get her so worked up that she made a reckless, impulsive decision to enter a contest she probably wouldn't even win. Mr. Gonzalez was right to say he couldn't count on her.

She felt like her son couldn't, either.

Looks like Santa couldn't come through with that gaming PC. Looks like not much of anything else, for that matter. Time to level with you, kid. Your asshole cousin was telling the truth.

Welp, there was nothing she could do about it. She'd made her choice and would have to live with it. She made it there. Time to see what this game was all about.

Rachel went back and forth whether she would be the one taking part in this game or if she would be sending Scarlett Saint in her stead. Ultimately, she opted for her alter ego.

Her thought process was with a five-million-dollar prize, it would not be easy to win. Despite that, Vortex was running the thing, so it was definitely going to be streamed on his site with millions of viewers. That could mean a ton of new subscribers! Even if she didn't win, she could still hedge the experience into a lucrative venture.

With that in mind, she selected her outfit strategically. Sexy was the goal, but she had no idea whether the contest would include physical challenges, so her clothing would need to be functional, just in case. That meant no skirts and no heels. That wouldn't be a problem.

She started with a matching red bra and G-string. The bra was sheer so her nipples would come out to play through her shirt. The top she chose was a tight, white, low-cut number that offered a tantalizing view of her ample cleavage. For whatever reason, the red didn't seem to show through. That was science for ya. Her leather pants were so tight they looked to be painted on, and her ass looked incredible if she did say so herself. The blinding white Nikes she wore matched her shirt and would serve her well if she had to do any running. Lastly, she slipped on a three-quarter-length leather jacket that wouldn't do shit to protect her from the cold, but it looked cute, and she only had to walk a short distance from her car to the mall.

She parked her BMW, another major expense of her lifestyle, next to a Ford pickup truck and a Kia sedan. When she stepped out, it was even colder than when she left her apartment forty-five minutes ago. Her nipples reacted immediately, and her shirt had the intended effect.

A woman ahead of her walked quickly toward the entrance, her pace likely to escape the cold given her worn winter jacket looked like it had seen better days. She must have sensed someone behind her, because she turned and met Rachel's eyes momentarily before continuing on her path.

The woman was maybe five or six years older than Rachel, but she had a tired look about her that made her look even older. If she styled her hair and slapped on some makeup, maybe put on some clothes that flattered her form, she would probably be quite attractive. She must have gone through some shit to end up looking that haggard. Sure, Rachel often lamented her life choices, but one look at this poor woman told her it could always be worse.

Rachel picked up her own pace—not trying to catch up with the woman, but to get out of the fucking cold. She was only a few feet from her when she reached the checkpoint where she saw the English guy who delivered the invitation to her, along with two big, scary-looking dudes. She tried to go straight into the mall, but one of the big men held up a hand for her to wait. They were inside the door. Why would she have to wait?

"Thank you, Mrs. Collins," she heard the sharp-dressed man say to the woman. "Please proceed to the concourse."

With the other woman heading inside, the man turned his attention to Rachel. "Ah! Miss—"

"Saint," she cut him off, while putting on her best sultry voice, hoping he was smart enough to understand she would be using her stage name tonight.

"I swear to god, if you cost me this opportunity, I'm going to be pissed!" Eléna whispered, chastising her roommate as they approached the mall entrance where the sharp-dressed man was standing, along with some large, scary-looking bodyguards. At least, she assumed they were bodyguards.

"And I'll be fucking furious if we both end up dead because you fell for this crazy scam!" Whitney whispered back with equal vitriol.

Damn it, Whit, why are you so stubborn?

Even though she was legitimately annoyed with her roommate, she had a point. This was more than a little sketchy, and no matter how enticing the prize, she wasn't going to let her go in there alone to face god knew what. If it resulted in a forfeit, that would just have to be that.

The sharp-dressed man's face curled into a frown when he saw Eléna's roommate accompanying her. "Miss Mendoza," he said, the pitch of his voice lower than she remembered. "You were given strict instructions to come alone. Who is this?"

Eléna answered while turning to glare at Whitney. "This is my roommate, who followed me here even though I assured her I was fine."

The man regarded the girls for a moment. He looked stern, like a principal about to hand down an expulsion. A pit developed in Eléna's stomach. She wasn't sure if it was because she was about to be disqualified or if it reminded her of her appointment at the registrar. Either way, it didn't feel good.

After a few interminably long moments, the man broke out into a laugh.

"That's commendable of you, Ms. Gamble," he said to Whitney.

Eléna's momentary relief at his shift to a more pleasant tone washed away when she realized he knew Whitney's last name.

From the look on her face, Whitney was thrown off as well.

The girls exchanged glances before looking up at the massive security guards on either side.

"Thanks," Whitney said, while still keeping her eye on the security guard to the man's left.

"Lucky for you, we have a few no shows, so we will allow you to takc part if you'd like. If not, you will both forfeit your chance at the prize."

The girls looked at each other again, and they came to the same conclusion. This situation was shady enough that they weren't concerned with losing out on the money. But something told them it wasn't going to be as easy as just walking away.

Steve was so busy staring at the college girls' asses as they walked in that he didn't notice Dom come up behind him.

The young mafioso grabbed the cop by the shoulder and spun him around. Steve saw Jimmy and Georgie, another of his guys, standing behind him.

"What the fuck you doing, Steve?" he asked. "You owe me over fifty K and you're shopping?"

Steve stepped back, releasing himself from Dom's

grip. "I'm getting your money, Dom. I still have until tomorrow."

Dom stepped up into Steve's face. "You'll have my money when I say you'll have my money, and I want it right fucking now!"

"Is there a problem, gentlemen?" a voice with a British accent interrupted.

The sharp-dressed man stood before them, flanked by two sizeable men. He looked annoyed.

"What's it to you, Jeeves?" Dom asked defiantly.

"Detective Bell is part of a contest we are holding here tonight. He was told to come alone, but it seems we have some problems with our participants' reading comprehension. The instructions emphasized *confidentiality*, yet two contestants in a row have disregarded that mandate." He turned to the man on his right. "Are they all taking the piss? I feel like I'm in one of Vortex's prank videos."

"I don't know nothing about that," Dom said. "I got business with this man, and it ain't none of yours, Alfred."

"Yes, your knowledge of stereotypical British butler names is quite impressive, Mister Capelli, but time is a factor here."

"How the fuck you know my name?" Dom asked as he reached into his jacket.

Dom was quick, but the bodyguards were quicker. Before he could even wrap his hands around the butt of his pistol, the big men each had their own trained on him.

"Whoa," he said as he slowly withdrew his hand from his jacket and held it back, gesturing for his guys to stand down. "Easy there, big fellas."

The sharp-dressed man continued as if he wasn't in danger of being in the middle of a firefight.

"Mr. Capelli," he said, not answering the question of just how exactly he knew who Dom was, "my employer, Vortex, is holding a contest here at this mall, where contestants have the opportunity to win five million dollars in cash. Detective Bell was an invited contestant. Typically, we'd turn the rest of you away, but we had two no-shows. One of the young ladies who walked in before you arrived has taken the first of those slots. Would you like to have the other?"

"Five million dollars? You're not fucking with me?"

"No, Mr. Capelli, I assure you I am not *fucking with you*."

He looked over at Jimmy and Georgie, who shrugged. They were muscle, not strategists. They weren't going to tell him if they were going to go through with it.

"Ok," Dom said, "let's do this."

"Splendid! I'll just need you to discard any weapons before entering the premises."

Dom narrowed his eyes, clearly uncomfortable with giving up his gun, but he complied. He pulled the Desert Eagle from his jacket slowly, not wanting to risk the ire of the bodyguards, who still had their own weapons trained on him. Flipping it so he was holding it by the barrel, he handed it to Jimmy, who tucked it into the back waistband of his pants.

"Satisfied?"

The man looked down toward Dom's shoes. "You'll need to give them the revolver in your ankle holster, as well. We'll also need your gun, Detective. Law enforcement or not, we do not allow anyone to bring weapons onto the premises."

Dom was too weirded out by the man's almost pre-cognitive ability to read people. He removed the snub-nosed .38 caliber from his ankle holster and handed it to Jimmy.

"Give Jimmy your piece, Steve."

"Fat chance," he said. "I'll lock it in my car."

"I'm afraid we're short on time, Detective. If you're not comfortable leaving your firearm with Mr. Capelli's people, you can give it to one of my associates here."

Steve wasn't thrilled with either option, but at least the guy had the air of a pro about him. Jimmy or Georgie would probably end up not giving his department-issued Glock back to him. He could see it used in a hit and implicating him.

Handing over his registered weapon to those guys wasn't ideal, either, but he sensed going back to the car would end up being a messy scenario, so he handed his gun to the bodyguard on the right.

"Thank you, Detective. You and Mr. Capelli can proceed inside, but Mr. Capelli's friends will need to remain outside."

"Wait in the car," Dom instructed. "C'mon, Steve, let's go win us some cash."

Jimmy and Georgie returned to the car, Jimmy in the driver's seat, Georgie on the passenger side. They started it up, and Frank Sinatra's smooth vocals filled the interior of the luxury vehicle. Jimmy was agitated and gripped the steering wheel as he leaned forward in thought.

"I don't like this," Jimmy said. "Maybe we should call Carmine."

"I don't know, man," Georgie said. "Dom ain't gonna like that."

"Yeah, well, Carmine's gonna like it even less if we let something happen to his boy. What do you think he's going to do to us?"

"You got a point," Georgie agreed. "That British guy was fucking we—"

He didn't get to finish the sentence because a long, curved, serrated blade pierced his left cheek. It was so sharp it pierced the flesh like butter. The knife slid through the interior of his mouth, catching his tongue and ripping into it, pinning it against the inside of his right cheek before it exited the other side, splashing the window with a gout of blood on the way out as the confused mobster let out a muffled scream.

Jimmy reached for his gun but, for the second time tonight, was too slow. A small hand with long, razor-sharp metal fingernails burst from the darkened backseat, driving them into his gut. The pain shot into his stomach and traveled up his esophagus so fast he thought he would vomit. In one swift motion, the assailant jerked their hand upward, opening a cavernous gash in his stomach. His mouth fell slack as blood flowed from it while he watched his guts sluice onto the leather seats.

While Jimmy was being eviscerated, the attacker pulled the knife out of Georgie's cheek, but only long enough to thrust it into his eye. As soon as it was embedded, they twisted it, obliterating the orb in its socket. Again, the assailant yanked the knife out, taking the remnants of Georgie's eyeball with it.

At the same time, they withdrew their claws from Jimmy's stomach and crossed their arms, the claw pressed against Georgie's throat and the knife against Jimmy's. They held them there for a split second before uncrossing their arms and drawing the blades across the goons' throats, unleashing a manic, high-pitched cackle as the arterial sprays painted the interior front windshield a bright shade of crimson.

Jimmy slumped in his seat, unable to move as the life drained out of him. Through the blood-spattered mirror, he got a good look at the woman in the backseat. She was disheveled, with ragged clothing and stringy, matted brown hair. The top of her face above her nose was covered in black greasepaint, which gave her green eyes an almost-ethereal glow. Several scars were embedded in her flesh, looking like an animal who had survived many a wilderness battle.

The last thing he saw before he died was the woman licking the blood off her blades.

CHAPTER 8

L ogan stood in line in the corridor leading to the concourse. There were two parallel groups waiting to sign the paperwork so the contest could begin. He looked around and assessed there were around fifty people there, not including the people running the operation. One thing that stood out to him was the variety of contestants. Old, young, short, tall, athletic, not-as-athletic, there was no one-specific trait the group shared. At least, not overtly.

Two men behind him were bickering. One was taller and of average build, wearing glasses, with short hair and a salt-and-pepper beard. The other was shorter, but more muscular, with tattooed arms and longish, dark hair. Both sported t-shirts with a logo depicting two cartoon vampires standing in front of a microphone. The text above the image read *Horror Movies and Shit*.

"I still don't know what we're doing here," the taller man said.

"Uh, we're trying to win money to take our podcast to the next level, Jim. Don't you want to bring your pedantic horror movie takes to a wider audience?"

"Better pedantic than pretentious, Mark!" Jim snapped back.

Logan rolled his eyes and was thankful he was next so

he didn't have to listen to them anymore.

A pleasant young woman sitting at the table handed him a form and a pen. He looked it over. Logan wasn't a legal expert, but it seemed to be a non-disclosure agreement. These things always seemed shady to him, but nothing he read jumped out at him as egregious.

"You want me to give you my phone?" he heard a woman ask from the direction of the adjacent line.

The woman was about Logan's age. She was attractive but wore the weight of what looked like years of stress. Her coat was unzipped, and she was wearing a red polo shirt with the Schow's Department Store logo and khaki pants. She must have skipped work to be there—the big box stores weren't in the habit of giving employees the night after Thanksgiving off.

"No phones are allowed during the contest, ma'am," the woman attending to the table said. "But they'll be safe in the lockbox until the contest is over."

The woman frowned and stepped aside, letting the girl behind her move ahead.

"I just have to text my babysitter. You can go."

The girl behind her was dressed for attention. Everything about her, from her low-cut white top and leather pants to the outrageous flame-red hair, screamed look at me. She was probably some kind of influencer.

"Name?" the woman working the table asked, a hint of disdain in her tone.

"Scarlett Saint," the woman proudly announced, looking around for a reaction. She didn't get one. Most in line were too busy checking their phones. Jim and Mark weren't scrolling through theirs, but Jim showed zero interest in the woman, and Mark was too busy badgering him about giving the film *Event Horizon* a six out of ten while claiming to love it. Pedantic and pretentious, indeed.

One guy toward the back, who looked like a Jersey Shore reject who had watched Goodfellas one too many times, seemed to be the only one actively eyeing her, but Logan didn't know if that was because he recognized her or because she was objectively attractive. He also wasn't sure if everyone else was trying to be subtle, while he didn't care if he looked like a creep.

"Not on the list," the worker said with a glare.

The redhead got flustered and lowered her voice, dropping the artificial sultriness and vocal fry. Logan wondered if she realized her normal speaking voice was infinitely more appealing.

"Uh, it's under Dubois. Rachel."

"Yup," the woman confirmed, handing her the NDA and pointing to the lockbox.

"Sign that. Phone here."

As she complied, Logan signed his form and handed it to the worker at his table.

"Phone?" she asked.

Logan turned out his pockets and the pouch of his hoodie.

"Didn't bring one."

That was true. He left his severely outdated Android device locked in his glove compartment. When he looked back at the other line, he saw the attention-seeker had moved on and the retail worker was back. She still looked frazzled as she signed her form and placed her own phone, also an older-model Android, in the lockbox.

They almost bumped into each other as they made their way around the intake tables, toward the concourse. Logan managed to stop at the last second.

"Oh," the woman blurted. "I'm so sorry!"

"No worries. After you, Kasey." The woman froze, and her anxiety was evident. Logan immediately felt bad for messing with her and pointed to the small bronze clip on her shirt. "Your name tag."

Her relief was instant, and she cracked a smile.

Logan found it endearing. To him, she was much more appealing than the redhead. He returned the smile politely, but he wasn't here to find a date. He was here to help a friend.

"Sorry," Kasey said, "I'm not even sure why I'm here. The people running this know way too much about me."

Logan's expression turned serious. She had momentarily disarmed him, but she was right. Whoever was running this thing had too much intel, far beyond your phone showing you an ad for something you had just been talking about. But these were desperate times, and looking at Kasey and the other contestants, he wasn't alone in them.

"Logan," he said, figuring the least he could do was let her know his own name.

"Nice to meet you, Logan," she said with a warm smile.

"That's Scarlett fucking Saint!" a voice excitedly whispered behind him.

He saw the Guido and another older guy walk past.

Everything about the older one told Logan he was a cop. Him walking with this Henry Hill wannabe made Logan suspect he was on the take.

"What's that supposed to mean?"

"Are you a fucking stunod? She's a porn star! I must have dropped a couple grand on her fan site this year! Maybe if I tell her, I can get a blowjob. Maybe I'll even

97

fuck her!"

"Yeah, and I'll bet you think strippers want to date you too."

The mob guy's expression twisted into anger. "You'd do well to remember who you're talking to, Steve-O. Just because you got a temporary reprieve don't mean you and me are square."

Logan sensed these two may be a problem. He would have to keep an eye out.

He walked alongside Kasey into the center of the concourse and was surprised at what he saw.

The mall had been shuttered for eighteen months, but you wouldn't know it. The lights were all on, including the marquees above the stores, which were all open, their interiors illuminated and shelves stocked. Escalators ran parallel in opposite directions up to and down from the second level. The faint sounds of nineties pop music droned from the speaker system, barely audible over the flow of water spouting from the pointed spire of the central fountain, the same one Logan would always toss a penny into on his way out.

To the side of the escalators was the only thing that wasn't a re-creation of the mall's heyday—a giant projector screen.

Logan turned back and saw everyone was gathered in the concourse area. A crew was breaking down the tables in the entryway behind a row of black-suited security guards who were blocking the exit.

Something was wrong here.

"Ladies and gentlemen," a voice with a British accent announced from the direction of the projector setup, "we ask that you kindly turn your attention to the screen."

The sharp-dressed man stood behind the podium. He

gave the crowd a few moments to stop murmuring and focus on the screen.

"Thank you, and welcome to our Black Friday Battle Royale! Without further ado, I present your host...Vortex!"

The room went dark as the screen lit up, showing a swirling, black pattern on a blood-red background. The swirling continued for several moments, accompanied by a buzz. It started as a minor irritation but increased in pitch and frequency, sounding as if a razor blade was being drawn across a cello string in front of a bullhorn. The sound, along with the eclectic pattern, created an unnerving atmosphere for the contestants.

Just when the sound felt like it had become interminable, it abruptly cut out and the image on the screen smash cut to a man wearing a full-face helmet with an LED screen playing a smaller version of the pattern that previously filled the entire screen.

The man in the helmet sat in a high-backed chair in front of a wall of monitors displaying high-definition images of various locations throughout the mall.

He had his hands folded in front of him as he leaned back in the chair, his index fingers extended and pressed together, forming a tent over his remaining folded digits. He wore a plain black turtleneck, similar to the style Steve Jobs made famous, and black leather gloves. The man remained silent for nearly a minute before he finally spoke.

"Welcome, contestants," he said in a deep, heavily-modulated voice. "I am Vortex. Some of you may know who I am. Others may not. That is not important. What is important is that each one of you was selected for the one thing you have in common—you all need money."

A smattering of whispers emanated from the crowd. Logan could make out a few words here and there, ranging from agreement to irritation to confusion.

"No shit."

"That's none of his business!"

"How does he know that?"

"Quiet, please," Vortex said, clearly able to hear the crowd on his end. "You will have the opportunity to ask questions when I'm finished."

The crowd fell silent again.

"As I was saying, you all have money troubles, and try as you may, you do not have the ability or aptitude to overcome them."

"Hey, fuck you, man!" a male voice from behind Logan shouted at the screen.

Vortex went silent but unclasped his hands and snapped his fingers. Immediately, two of the security guards approached a man who looked to be in his thirties and appeared average in every way, from his appearance to his outfit.

"Mr. Powell," Vortex said, "your anger is misplaced. I'm not the one who told you to gamble away your children's college funds in Atlantic City. I'm simply giving you an opportunity to not only win it back, but to send them to any college in the world. However, one more rude outburst and I will disqualify you and have my men escort you out. Do you understand?"

"Y... Yes," the man stammered.

"Good. That goes for everyone else too. Any further interruptions will be met with disqualification. Understood?" He paused and let the crowd's silence answer for them.

"Now, as I was saying, you all have financial worries, but the contents of my briefcases can make those worries disappear!"

He snapped his fingers again, and five drop-dead gorgeous women made their way around the screen. Each was adorned in short, black, cleavage-baring cocktail dresses and stiletto heels. Each also carried a briefcase. It reminded Logan of the game shows of old, pumping up the sex appeal to draw in male viewers.

The girls lined up in front of the screen and held out their briefcases, popping them open to show the awestruck crowd the contents.

"Each of these cases contains the sum of one million dollars. Five cases. Five million dollars in total. No check. No taxes. You can keep every red cent."

An air of excitement washed over most of the crowd, but some, Kasey in particular, looked decidedly less so.

"This seems too good to be true," she whispered, more in general than to Logan.

"It is," Logan whispered back, eyeing the wall of muscle blocking the exit.

"Before I explain how you win, I want to let you know the most important thing you'll need to consider when it comes to strategy." He took a pause Logan assumed was for dramatic effect. "The most important thing is to understand there are five prizes, which means there can be a maximum of five winners. However, if you are willing to go further than your opponents, one of you can take home the entire five million dollars. It's simply a matter of how far you will go to win it all."

"This is crazy!" an older man near the perimeter shouted. He looked to be in his sixties, with a bad toupee and a substantial gut. "I didn't sign up for this!"

"Well, then, Mr. Bradley, you're free to leave, along with anyone else who doesn't have the stomach to participate," Vortex announced to the crowd's surprise.

Again he snapped his fingers, and the security detail blocking the exit stepped aside, leaving the path to the exit unimpeded.

Mr. Bradley didn't hesitate to start powerwalking toward the doors. After a few stunned beats, some of the crowd followed behind.

Kasey took a step in that direction, but Logan grabbed her arm and held her back. She spun to face him, more confused than angry. Logan offered a slight head shake and whispered a reminder of what she said earlier.

"Too good to be true."

She nodded her understanding, the fear in her eyes clear.

Mr. Bradley broke into a jog about halfway down the hall toward the exit, the rest of the crowd that wanted out a few paces behind him. The rest of the contestants who shared Logan's belief that it wasn't as simple as Vortex just letting them leave watched in nervous anticipation.

The cop and the crook, along with the podcasters, pushed their way past two girls who looked to be college students. Mob guy stopped long enough to tell the red-haired influencer she should leave too, but she stayed back, along with the college girls.

A wave of relief washed over the group as the doors opened automatically once Mr. Bradley got close enough to trigger the sensors. But that relief was short-lived.

As soon as the doors slid open, a loud bang echoed from the distance. A split-second later, the back of Mr. Bradley's head exploded in a shower of blood, skull fragments, and brain matter.

The dead man fell onto his back, his shattered cranium breaking open even more as it smashed directly into the tile.

The portion of the crowd trying to flee stopped moving forward and dropped to the ground. Some covered their heads as blood pooled around Mr. Bradley's corpse, chunks of gore floating in the rapidly spreading puddle.

Logan had also ducked, instinctively pulling Kasey down with him and shielding her with his body. He could feel her heaving as she released rapid, panicked breaths.

"Stay down," he whispered as he watched the security detail move on the group in the entryway. They had their pistols drawn as they pulled people off the floor, ordering them back to the concourse.

More security emerged from the other side of the projector, the same direction the models with the briefcases had come from. This group was dressed the same, but instead of pistols, they were armed with MP5 submachine guns.

Frightened screams echoed through the concourse as the crowd was herded back together. A few of Vortex's men fired their guns into the air, spurring the unwitting contestants into silence.

"I forgot to mention that there are snipers posted at every exit. Once you are down to the final five—or less—you'll be free to walk out and collect your prize. If you try to escape before then, you'll end up like poor Mr. Bradley over there."

The crowd remained in a stunned silence, no one daring to interrupt their sadistic host further.

"Now, I know what you're thinking," the masked man said. "You'll just wait it out until the authorities come looking for you. That would be a solid plan, except for one minor detail—the mall is rigged with a massive amount of explosives that are set to detonate at exactly two a.m. That's two hours from now, in case you suffer from time blindness."

"You can't do this!" the cop shouted. "People know we're here!"

"The rules explicitly stated that you were to tell no one about the contest. Now, I know some of you disregarded this, but no one you told will come looking for you or tell anyone else about this."

"What the fuck does that mean?" Mr. Powell shouted, a distinctive panic in his voice.

"It means, Mr. Powell, that..." Vortex said before trailing off and contemplating something for a moment. "You know, let me show you. I'll be honest, most of you complied. However, Mr. Powell and Mrs. Abernathy both let the existence of this game slip. Mr. Powell told his wife and two children, while Mrs. Abernathy told her son."

Logan looked to see the face of an approximately seventy-year-old woman turn a ghostly shade of white.

Suddenly, Vortex disappeared and was replaced by a split screen of what looked like grainy surveillance footage.

On the left, a woman and two pre-teen children—a boy and a girl—were tied up and seated on a couch in what looked like the average suburban living room. They were gagged and looked absolutely terrified. Behind each hostage stood a man holding a hunting knife to each of their throats. They wore ski masks, making them unidentifiable.

"Claire!" Mr. Powell screamed. "You motherfucker!"

"Watch your language, Mr. Powell," the sharp-dressed

man said as his boss's proxy. "You wouldn't want our associates to slip, would you? Those knives look quite sharp."

"No," Powell said helplessly.

On the other screen, a middle-aged man in what looked to be a delivery-driver's uniform was kneeling on a wooden dock. He was also gagged, with his hands tied behind his back. Like the Powell family, a man dressed all in black and wearing a ski mask stood behind him. Only this man was holding a pistol affixed with a silencer to the shaking man's head.

Vortex's voice came back while the awful images remained on the screen.

"It was a simple direction that you couldn't follow. My rules carry consequences to breaking them. Like this."

Once again, the masked maniac snapped his fingers. The snap was followed by Mr. Powell's and Mrs. Abernathy's worst nightmares playing out on the screen.

Mrs. Abernathy fainted, while Mr. Powell screamed and fell to his knees, falling into a fetal position.

Kasey looked away a second before Vortex's men completed their grisly deeds. She turned into Logan, surprising him initially, but he put his arm around her while she buried her face in his hoodie. He had seen some horrific shit in wartime. Barbarism for barbarism's sake. What happened reminded him of that.

"Let's recap," Vortex said. "Five cases. Five million dollars. Walk out with everyone else dead before two a.m. and you win. Fail to eliminate your opponents in time, and the building explodes, killing all of you. Try to escape before the contest ends, and my snipers eliminate you."

"What the hell do you get out of this?" someone

shouted.

"What do I always get?" Vortex replied with a laugh. "Views. I have a very special audience for events like this. They pay a lot of money just for the privilege of viewing. Add in betting on who will win, and this will be quite a lucrative evening for my company."

"And you're just going to cover all of this up?" the cop yelled.

"I bought this mall months ago. I'm demolishing to build luxury houses. All evidence will be gone, and you all will just be among the sad missing-person statistics that plague this country. And yes, I know you're thinking—what if the winners have a crisis of conscience? Let's just say that if the money doesn't motivate them, I think I've more than proven we can find them and deal with them if they try to talk."

Again the crowd fell silent, save for the weak sobs of Mr. Powell.

The sharp-dressed man looked at his watch. Logan parroted the movement and saw it was 11:57 p.m., three minutes until Black Friday.

The man signaled to Vortex's goons, and they formed a circle around him and escorted him out through the crowd, which parted as they made their way through. He took a moment and stopped above Mr. Powell, reaching into his pocket and dropping a handkerchief next to the devastated man who had just seen his family murdered.

"Rules are rules, Mr. Powell," he said coldly as he left the building with the rest of the security detail.

A rising tension permeated the concourse as people started looking around, sizing each other up. Some wondered if they could go through with it, while others were practically licking their chops to get started.

Logan looked to Kasey, who was shaking in fear at what was about to happen. "Stick with me," he told her. "Keep your head down and follow my lead."

"Why...why should I trust you?"

"You don't have a choice," he said bluntly.

He looked back down at his watch just in time to see it tick the stroke of midnight.

On cue, a siren sounded and all hell broke loose.

PART II

LET THE
GAMES BEGIN!

CHAPTER 9

T he violence started immediately. Not everyone was quick to attack, but enough of the panicked contestants started in on each other to spur the rest to fight back.

Mr. Powell was the first, and most obvious, target. Otto, a burly man with a bald, tattooed head and a long, dark beard wearing a biker vest that said Hell's Horde M.C., Trenton, NJ, pounced on him. Otto lived a life of violence, violence that would be inflicted on him if his club knew he stole money from them, so he didn't hesitate. He raised a steel-toed boot and drove it directly down on the man's head, caving in the side of his temple. The devastated husband and father with a gambling problem might not have even registered it as the impact popped his eyeball out of his skull. The biker raised his foot and slammed it down again, this time catching his nose and crushing the cartilage as a gout of blood sprayed the tile. Several more stomps followed, even after the man was dead.

A few feet away, a thin, shaky woman named Debbie, with yellowed teeth and track marks lining her exposed arms, had her hands wrapped around Mrs. Abernathy's neck, her knuckles white with the effort. Debbie's story wasn't complicated. She was a junkie and had no money to support her habit and no family or friends to help her through it. The old woman's face turned blue as she woke from her fainting spell, trying in vain to fight off the frail but younger woman. It didn't take long for her to stop struggling as she fell back, her tongue lolling out of her mouth.

Some of the group tried to escape rather than fight. Seth, a man in his late thirties who had never been in a fight a day in his life, bolted for the escalator. His unfiled tax returns and the IRS breathing down his neck didn't seem as pressing a problem in that moment as it did an hour before.

Jared, a gym bro in his mid-twenties whose ill-advised supplement-shop venture was about to go out of business, caught up to him with no problem and tackled him just as he stepped onto the moving stairway.

Seth fought and clawed to get out from under him, but Jared was just too strong. He grabbed Seth by his hair and slammed his head into the steps, the clawed edge cutting his forehead on impact. Seth screamed in anguish as his assailant lifted him back up, his scalp tearing as his hair was yanked back.

The younger man continued to pound Seth's face into the escalator as it ascended. Jared stopped pulling his victim's face back as they neared the top and, instead, held it down as the steps disappeared into the mechanism. The older man let out one final, defeated wail as the front of his face was ripped from his skull and slid under the top of the escalator. Jared dragged the body away from the instrument of death and looked to make sure he was dead. He looked at the exposed muscle of the man's ruined, bloody face and pushed the body back down the escalator, watching it tumble limply to the first floor.

With one man down, Jared turned and saw Leslie, a woman a few years older than him, running toward the food court, which was at the top of the second-floor concourse. Bloodlust in his eyes, he followed her into a door behind a burger stand. It led to a kitchen which, unfortunately for him, was still functional. Leslie grabbed a basket from a fryer full of boiling oil and flung the contents into Jared's face.

His skin burned and melted upon impact. He brought his hands up in an attempt to wipe the scalding grease from his face, but all that did was pull the liquefied flesh from his face in a gooey mess of gore. He screamed, not unlike the man he killed on the escalator, before Leslie put him out of his misery by jamming a butcher knife into his throat.

Leslie never imagined she could murder someone, but she also never figured she would manage to run up $80,000 in credit card debt behind her husband's back. But there she found herself.

With another contestant out of the way, Leslie ran back toward the concourse and looked down at the people fighting below. She thought maybe she could hang out where she was and hide until the numbers thinned out, but Otto had made his way up to the second floor thinking the same thing. He grabbed Leslie by the nape with one hand and her belt with the other. He pulled her back and used her momentum to toss her over the side of the railing. She tumbled end over end and landed on the spire of the fountain. The ceramic point shattered her spine as it pierced through her back and out her stomach, a rope of intestine wrapping around the spire as her body slid down the length, coming to a stop halfway to the bottom, the blood pouring into the fountain and turning the crystal-blue water crimson.

Toward the center of the concourse, Jim, Mark, Eléna, Whitney, and Rachel all formed a protective circle, but luckily for them, the other contestants were engaged in either their own battles or their attempts to hide.

"We gotta get the fuck out of here!" Jim shouted.

"Brilliant plan, Jim!" Mark shot back. "Any ideas?"

Jim surveyed his surroundings, and something caught his attention.

"There!" he said, pointing at a store called Lee's Sporting Goods. "We can hide out in there and grab some bats or something!"

Mark considered it but had an idea of his own.

"That car!" he said, pointing a hundred yards down the concourse to a sports car. He wasn't sure what the model was, but it stood next to a big, obnoxious sign that said *Win This Car*! "We can drive out of here."

"Are you fucking nuts?" Rachel shouted. "The snipers will take us out!"

"Not if we go fast enough!" Mark said. "Better than trying to fight through all these fuckers!"

"She's right," Eléna chimed in. "We're better off taking shelter and figuring out our next move."

"Do what you want!" Mark shouted. "I'm getting the fuck out of here."

With that, he ran down the concourse.

"Mark, don't fucking do it!" Jim shouted after him, but he either didn't hear or ignored him.

Mark made it to the car, finding it hard to believe how good his luck was that no one else thought of it. Even more luckily, the keys were in the ignition!

Serves Jim's pedantic ass right! Mark thought as he

turned the key and put the car in drive. He immediately gunned it back, toward the concourse, planning to take the hard left and slam through the doors to freedom. He didn't care how good those snipers were. They wouldn't hit him if he moved fast enough.

He was so wrapped up in his plan he didn't hear the timer start as soon as he started the car. It was three seconds, and he was still thirty yards away from the crowd brawling in the center, when the bomb in the trunk exploded. The force expelled him through the window, the shards ripping into his face and tattooed arms as he flew. Both the airtime and velocity were impressive as he met a spectacular end when his face slammed into the ledge of the second floor, caving in on impact, sending a shower of blood and teeth to the floor below as his lifeless body followed with a hearty splat.

He almost landed directly on Kasey, but Logan pulled her out of the way just in time. She didn't know why she gravitated toward this man, but there was something about him. In a situation like this, where she couldn't trust anybody, he at least had protected her by keeping her from trying to leave, saving her a swift death from a sniper's bullet. He saved her from getting crushed by a falling corpse when he could have let her die and had one less opponent to contend with.

To her right, Jessica, a beautiful woman in her early forties with a mountain of medical bills, slammed a stool into the back of Carl's head. Carl, also in his forties, was an aspiring writer whose horror novels weren't exactly raking in Stephen King money. He crumpled to the floor as Jessica pounced on him. She immediately sunk her teeth into his neck and pulled back, taking a huge chunk of flesh with her as the arterial spray soaked her pink shirt that, ironically, read *Be Kind*.

On Kasey's left, Owen, an aspiring professional wrestler fed up with making fifty bucks a weekend and sleeping in his car, was using Vortex's projector to obliterate the face of Thomas, a wealthy investor whose bottom line was seriously diminished by his two ex-wives, who had each taken him to the cleaners. There was nothing left of his face, just a gory husk of chunked flesh and shattercd bone, as Owen's roid rage fueled his murderous act.

Otto, the MVP of this contest thus far, ran up behind Owen with a meat cleaver absconded from the food court. He thrust the blade into the side of Owen's neck, and copious amounts of blood spurted from the gash. He raised and swung the cleaver several more times, until Owen's head tumbled from his shoulders and landed next to Thomas's corpse. Otto laughed as Owen's headless body stayed on its knees.

Kasey saw the whole thing and also saw he had his eye on Logan next.

"Logan! Look out!"

Logan turned just in time to see the big biker charging him, cleaver raised high and ready to strike.

The swing was wild, and Logan sidestepped it, the blade making a whooshing sound as it cut through the air, missing its intended target. He responded by punching the biker in the throat, causing him to drop his weapon as he clutched his neck for air.

While they were distracted, Vito, whose pizzeria was about two weeks from going under, came up behind Kasey and spun her around. He put his hands around her throat and squeezed. She managed to choke out Logan's name again just before the air left her lungs.

Logan took his attention away from Otto and started toward Kasey, but the outlaw recovered quickly and speared Logan from behind, knocking the wind out of him as he slammed into the floor. Otto started raining blows on the back of Logan's head, using his bulky forearms as clubs. Logan put his hands on the back of his head to protect from the onslaught, but too many of the strikes were landing as intended.

Kasey gripped Vito's wrists and tried to pull them away, but he was too strong. He pushed her down over the edge of the fountain, and she felt her hair get wet as her head dipped into the water. She dug her fingernails into his hairy arms, tearing into the flesh, but he held on.

She saw Logan was also in trouble, as the biker was beating the holy hell out of him directly to her right. They were close. She just hoped they were close enough as she kicked her leg toward Otto, catching him with a glancing blow under his eye. It wasn't a big impact, but it was enough to stagger him, giving Logan the opening he needed.

Using all his strength, Logan pushed up off the ground, sending his off-balance opponent reeling away from him. He spun and delivered a haymaker that struck Otto directly in his jaw. A jab to the nose following that made the biker's eyes water as his head struck the tile. Logan mounted him and jammed his thumbs into Otto's eyes, crushing the orbs as gouts of blood exploded from the sockets. He wasn't dead yet, but he was off the board.

Kasey was in real trouble. Vito had her head entirely submerged while continuing to strangle her. Logan rushed behind him and wrapped his arm around Vito's neck, pulling him back. Vito lost his grip on Kasey's neck but tried to grab her polo shirt, ripping it open but also helping pull her from the water. Her hands went to her bruised throat as she heaved and gasped to replenish her lost air.

Vito struggled against Logan, but he was much stronger than Kasey. Fucking piece of shit was preying on those weaker than him? He deserved what was about to happen. Logan bellowed as he squeezed and twisted his arm, snapping Vito's neck. He let the body slump to the floor next to Otto, who was writhing in pain, blood pouring through his fingers as he covered his ruined eye sockets.

"Are you okay?" Logan asked Kasey as he put his arm around her, helping her walk as she continued her attempts to regain a normal breathing rhythm. She nodded, not wanting to risk the pain of talking.

Logan surveyed the battlefield, never in his life having thought a shopping mall would become what he saw in Afghanistan. Blood, gore, and broken bodies littered the concourse. Some still fought. Others ran for their lives. By his estimation, at least half the contestants were dead or severely wounded. The battle was going to continue, but if they had any hope of making it through, they would have to regroup.

Logan saw a path leading away from the concourse that looked open. There were a few bloody corpses but no one actively fighting or blocking.

He grabbed Kasey by the hand and led her toward safety.

CHAPTER 10

L ogan slammed his hand down on the gate controls as soon as he and Kasey ducked inside Keene's Department Store. He breathed a sigh of relief at the groan and clank of the mechanism as the metal gate descended.

With a bloodthirsty mob tearing itself apart inside the mall, snipers waiting to pick off anyone on the outside, and the minor matter of bombs set to level the building in less than two hours, they were nowhere near safe, but finding time to regroup and figure out a strategy was critical.

He ushered Kasey away from the entrance, toward the back of the store. The gate was a barrier, but not a sturdy one. And it definitely didn't make them invisible, so it was in their interest to move away.

They made their way to the housewares section and ducked behind a shelf out of site. Logan grabbed a dish towel, grimacing as he pressed it to the back of his head.

When he pulled it away, it was soaked with blood, which wasn't surprising given the pounding pain he felt from Otto bouncing it off the floor like a basketball.

"Jesus!" Kasey said when she saw the blood. "Let me look."

Logan went to protest, but he was too late as Kasey

put her hand on his back and nudged him forward so she could get a better look.

As she focused on examining his injury, she stopped holding her torn shirt and it fell open, exposing her chest and stomach, a plain white bra the only thing protecting her modesty.

She noticed Logan avert his eyes and immediately became self-conscious. Her skin flushed as red as her ruined garment. She used one hand to hold it closed while examining Logan's scalp with the other.

Logan couldn't help a slight smirk. They had just escaped a chaotic riot where many people had been brutally killed, yet they were sitting like awkward teenagers because of a torn shirt.

"Hold on," Logan said as he pulled off his hoodie, being careful around his head. He handed it to Kasey, leaving him in his cutoff Metallica t-shirt, exposing his muscled arms. "Here."

Kasey smiled warmly at the chivalrous gesture and surprised Logan by taking off her shirt as if all her embarrassment had abruptly vanished. It wasn't meant to entice. It was more an acknowledgment of the growing trust between them. She immediately replaced it with the hoodie and said, "Thank you," before adding, "let's get a look at that head."

Logan leaned forward, head down and elbows resting on his thighs as Kasey used the towel to gently dab away the blood around the wound.

"You've got a gentle touch," he told her.

"Yeah, well, that's the thing about being a boy mom," she said. "You're all so quick to throw caution to the wind, but all that rough and tumble goes out the window when you get hurt and run back to Mommy to make it better."

Logan laughed. "You're not wrong."

"Marine?" she asked.

Logan would have wondered how she assumed that, but given what she had seen him do out there, he wasn't surprised. He was even less surprised since the eagle, globe, and anchor tattoo on his right arm was exposed without his hoodie.

"Yup."

"My father-in-law served. I could tell by the way you carried yourself, even before I saw your tattoo. He had the same one."

"How about your husband?" Logan asked, regretting the words as soon as they came out, especially when he saw Kasey's expression immediately stiffen. "Sorry. Too personal."

Kasey shook it off. "No, it's fine. He died a long time ago. I'm just...it's been a long time since anyone's asked about him." Her eyes were watering.

"I'm sorry."

Kasey nodded as she tossed aside the bloody towel and grabbed a fresh one from the shelf. She pressed it against the wound gently but held it in place.

"His dad was this hard-nosed military guy. He never said it, but I think he was secretly disappointed that his son became a teacher. Like he wasn't strong or something."

"There are other ways to be tough besides being on the battlefield."

Kasey sniffled. "Yeah. And tough doesn't always get you out alive."

"No, it doesn't." He offered his own personal anecdote in return for Kasey's candor. "My best friend is the toughest son of a bitch I ever met. Me and him should've died ten times over during our tours in the Middle East. He survived all that only to end up with lung cancer once he gets out."

"I'm sorry," Kasey said.

"I'm sorry about your husband," Logan said.

"Yeah. Me too. But I got my son out of it. Every time I miss Liam, I look at our son and I see that he's still with me."

"That's nice. Must be a special kid."

"He is. He's the reason I did this stupid contest. All he wants is a stupid fucking gaming PC. I can't afford it. I figured if I could win some money, I could finally give him a good Christmas." Kasey rolled her eyes.

"You sound like a good mom," Logan said, watching her blush at the compliment.

"Thank you." Kasey felt a small smile on her lips.

They locked eyes. There was something there. Whether it was a bond forged on this unlikely battlefield or some type of deeper attraction was a question that would need to wait.

"We gotta stop that bleeding," she said, breaking the silence. "I think you need stitches."

Logan looked around.

"I'm sure we can cobble something together." He pointed to a sign that read Hardware. "That should do."

He started toward the sign, but Kasey grabbed his arm to stop him.

"I've got a better idea," she said. "This place isn't that different from the store I wo...used to work for. There's gotta be an office somewhere. And it should have a proper first aid kit."

"Guess that's better than glue and duct tape. Let's go."

As they started toward the back of the store, hoping to find the office, Logan heard something behind them. It was faint, but it sounded like someone trying to move lightly but stepping just a hair too heavy to be soundless.

Logan spun on his heels and stepped in front of Kasey. "We're not alone."

"What the fuck was that?" Rachel exclaimed once the shutters descended, blocking off the entrance to the sporting goods store.

"That was fucking insane," Jim acknowledged as he hunched over and braced himself on his knees while he caught his breath.

Rachel and Jim, along with Eléna and Whitney, had made a break for the sporting goods store at the same time Mark was meeting his untimely demise. Fortunately—or unfortunately, depending on how you looked at it—many other contestants were still locked in battle or dead, allowing the quartet to reach a safe haven.

"You going to be okay?" Whitney asked Jim.

Jim stood upright and put his hands on his hips, taking one more deep breath before it slowed to a manageable pace.

"I'm fine," he said, looking around the store. "Lots of stuff we could use in here."

Eléna pulled an aluminum baseball bat from a rack on the wall. "Definitely more useful than anything we'd find at Bath and Body Works."

"This is a pretty big place," Jim said. "There's an escalator over there, so it's probably got stuff on both floors. We should pair up just in case anyone else snuck in before us." He turned to Rachel. "Red, why don't you come with me upstairs, while you ladies look around down here?"

"Yeah, no," Rachel said snidely. "I'm not convinced I should trust you, either. How do I know you aren't some kind of pervert?"

"Don't flatter yourself, sweetie," Jim clapped back. "You're not my type."

"I'm everyone's type," Rachel said defiantly. "And it's Scarlett."

Jesus, talk about Main Character Syndrome, Eléna thought.

"Fine. Whitney, you go with Red."

"Scarlett," Rachel said again, her attitude meter set to maximum.

"Scarlett?" Eléna mimicked sarcastically. "Didn't you say your name was Rebecca or something in line?"

"It's Rachel," she said. "But I prefer Scarlett."

"Whatever," Eléna said, turning back to Whitney. "You and Scarlett go downstairs, and Jim and I will look around here. Cool?"

Whitney didn't look thrilled, but this wasn't a staff meeting. It was life or death, and they didn't have time to fuck around.

"Sure," she said.

"Fine," Rachel said, rolling her eyes.

Jim shrugged. "Good with me."

"Let's go, Rachel," Whitney said, purposely using the girl's government name to irritate her as she walked toward the stairs.

Rachel looked infuriated but kept her mouth shut as she stomped after her.

Eléna and Jim couldn't help but smirk at the model's mini tantrum, despite the circumstances.

"You're not going to attack me, right?"

"Sorry, sweetie, you're not my type, either."

As they tried to escape the melee, Dom bumped into Otto, the blind biker who was stumbling around trying to get his bearings. When Dom made contact, the burly man immediately wrapped his hands around Dom's throat and started choking him. He couldn't see, but he was still strong as hell, and Dom couldn't break his grip.

Fortunately, Steve saw him in trouble and came up behind Otto and kicked him in the balls. The large, sightless man fell to his knees, where Dom kicked him square in the face, smashing his nose.

"This way!" Steve said, pointing to a sign that listed several locations throughout the mall, with arrows pointing the directions. The one he was interested in read Security.

Part of him thought he should have let Dom die. But

that would have only solved an immediate problem. Jimmy and Georgie knew they were both in here. If Steve made it out alive and Dom didn't, they would hold him responsible, even if he wasn't the one who killed him. So on top of trying to keep himself alive, he was also responsible for the safety of Carmine's psychotic, dipshit son.

"Smart move, Steve-O," Dom said with a smug smile.

We'll see, Steve thought. Dom was impulsive and, in his estimation, not very smart. Yes, it was in his best interests to keep the young mobster alive, but the mook could also easily get them both killed. Steve knew he would need to be smart, cautious, and, most of all, lucky to get out of there breathing.

The men broke away from the chaos, which was dying down. Literally.

There were more broken, bloody bodies on the floor than people standing upright battling not to join the carpet of corpses.

Steve kept looking back over his shoulder until they turned into the alcove leading to the security room.

He kept watch, while Dom checked the door. It didn't take long for him to shout, "God damn motherfucking cocksucking piece of fucking shit!" He kicked the metal door in a frustrated rage.

Steve grabbed him and pulled him back. The last thing he needed was to have to get the jackass out of there alive with a broken foot.

"Chill the fuck out, Dom!" Steve yelled as he pulled him back far enough that the young mobster's last kick only found air. "Let me look!"

"Vaffuncolo!" Dom exclaimed as he tried to compose himself.

Steve looked at the keypad to the right of the door.

It had the numbers zero through nine, letters A through D, and four directional keys. A note above it read:

You think you're safe? On the CONTRAry, you would struggle to survive even if you had THIRTY LIVES. If only you had some type of CHEAT CODE...

"What the fuck does that mean?" Dom asked.

Steve ignored him. It wasn't hard to figure out. There were portions of or whole words capitalized. That was intentional. *CONTRA. THIRTY LIVES. CHEAT CODE.*

A smile cracked Steve's face. He understood.

"This Vortex guy plays video games, right?"

"I guess so. The fuck's that got to do with anything?"

Steve wouldn't know if this clue had anything to do with modern games. All that *Grand Theft Call of Duty* crap. But this was different.

Steve hadn't touched a controller in over thirty years, but back in 1987, at fourteen years old, his favorite game was Contra for the original Nintendo. The game was fun but hard as shit, impossible to beat with only the three lives the game granted you. The developers clearly knew this, because they programmed a cheat code—a series of button presses that, when entered on the title screen, would give the player thirty lives.

Whether this Vortex fucker knew Steve would remember the code or if it was just a random puzzle for anyone to find would have to remain an unanswered question, assuming it actually worked.

He started the input. His muscle memory for it surprised him. It had been three decades since he last entered it on his controller, sitting on the royal-blue carpet in front of the nineteen-inch television in his parents' living room in the Chambersburg section of

Trenton.

Up, up, down, down, left, right, left, right, B, A, enter.

The last button pressed on the controller was the start button, but there wasn't a button with that label on the keypad, so he hoped Enter would do the trick. It did.

The door clicked, and Steve turned the handle, relief flooding through him as the door opened. He stepped aside to let Dom in, and he reached out to tear the note with the clue off the wall before closing and locking the door behind them.

Steve would have appreciated a minute to catch his breath and think, but he saw Dom make a break for one side of the long metal table in the center of the room. There was a .38-caliber revolver on either side.

The table was too big for either of them to grab both guns at the same time. Dom probably thought he could run around and grab both before Steve realized what was happening.

The older man was a step slower, but he wasn't that slow. He made it to the opposite end of the table and grabbed the other weapon, immediately training it on Dom, who put his hands up but didn't drop his own gun.

"Whoa, Steve-O," he said, as if he didn't understand why the detective was being aggressive. "What are we doing here?"

"You're the one running for the first weapon you saw, Dom."

He shrugged. "I got excited. Sue me."

"Excited, huh?"

"Yeah. We got weapons now. That automatically gives us an advantage over the rest of these fucks." He got serious. "Look, Steve, me and you got beef, no doubt. But we both got a shared problem with this Vortex guy and these assholes trying to kill each other. And us."

The guy wasn't the brightest bulb, but he had a point.

"So, what do you want to do?"

Steve knew what they should do. And he was relatively sure Dom would agree, but his question was strategic. He had to let Dom think he was in charge. Like it or not, he had to not only get Dom out of there alive, but he also had to find his way into the mobster's good graces. If not, Steve may as well turn the gun on himself right then.

Steve looked around. The room they were in was bare outside of the table and another door on the opposite wall. In a lot of ways, it looked like an interrogation room. He cocked his head toward the door.

"If I lower my gun, will you keep yours down?"

"Yeah, Steve. I will."

Steve lowered his gun, half-expecting to raise it again, but Dom kept his word. He popped the cylinder and confirmed it was loaded with bullets in all six chambers.

"Yours loaded?"

Dom opened the cylinder of his own pistol. "Yeah."

"Alright, let's see what's on the other side of that door."

Steve moved to one side of the door, while Dom flanked the other. They each raised their guns, but not at each other, as Steve turned the handle. This door was unlocked, and it opened without impediment when Steve pushed it in.

Had Dom been a competent partner, he would have gone in and cleared the room before Steve, but he hung back like a chooch and waited for the detective to take the lead.

Steve spun and aimed his gun toward each corner of the room, making sure it was empty. Dom moved in behind him, holding his gun out like he was Jack Bauer or something. It was easy to be brave knowing there was no immediate danger.

"Whoa, look at this fucking place," Dom said with a whistle as he eyed the wall of monitors. Each displayed a different camera angle of the mall. Steve had seen plenty of security rooms over the course of his career, but that was something else entirely. It was exactly what they needed if they were going to escape the place. But it seemed too good to be true.

"This ain't normal," Steve said. "Too good to be true."

"Ain't nothing about this normal," Dom said. "But we gotta use whatever advantage we can get."

He wasn't wrong.

"Looks like there aren't many people left," Steve remarked.

As he looked over the camera, he saw the concourse was mostly clear, of the living anyway. A few stragglers were stumbling around, some in really bad shape with bloody faces and obviously broken bones. They were mainly trying to get into the shuttered stores for whatever respite they could find.

"Maybe we can find an opening to get out of here," Steve commented as his eyes darted from monitor to monitor.

"I don't see Scarlett," Dom said, ignoring his partner's idea.

"What?"

"Scarlett Saint, the hot chick with the red hair. I don't see her body." He nudged Steve with his elbow, as if prompting him to laugh. "And I'd recognize that body anywhere!"

Is this guy fucking serious? Steve thought. "So what, Dom?"

"So maybe she needs our help. Maybe she'd be grateful to get it."

"You gotta be kidding me." Steve couldn't believe what he was hearing.

"Relax, Steve-O. I'm not saying we go out looking for her, but if she pops up on one of these monitors and she ain't too far away...I'm just saying. It'd be the gentlemanly thing to do." Dom's face was lit up like a fifteen-year-old with his first *Playboy*.

Jesus Christ, he's going to get us killed, isn't he?

"Let's just focus on getting out of here alive, ok?" Steve said. "A couple million dollars will get you a bunch of Scarlett Saints."

"Sure," Dom said. "Let's find a way out of this fucking mall."

CHAPTER 11

Vortex smiled at the carnage on his monitors. He had started with over fifty contestants, and from what he could see on the monitors, he was down to nineteen. There had been some spectacular kills along the way. His personal favorites were the face shredding on the escalator, the woman impaled on the fountain spire, and Mark's explosive expulsion from the car.

He had to admit he was a little disappointed more people hadn't sprung his traps, but there was still time for that.

The phone rang. There was no caller ID. All his devices were burners. He knew who the caller was immediately, as only one person had that number.

"Wesley," he said as he answered.

"Sir," a man with a British accent said, "I trust you are satisfied with the performance thus far?"

"Oh yes," Vortex said. "The crew has been moved, other than the snipers?"

"Yes, sir. And the clean-up crew is on standby after the finale."

"Perfect," he replied. Wesley was an excellent coordinator, worth every penny.

Wesley was the one who facilitated it all for him. He set up the shell companies to purchase the abandoned shopping mall. He also prepared and presented dossiers on the contestants, identifying people desperate enough to show up for the chance to solve their money problems.

Of course, all he needed to do was get them there. Once inside, they were locked in. The world-class mercenaries Vortex enlisted would make sure of that. Wesley also did a spectacular job of monitoring them in the week leading up to the contest, making sure they kept it confidential and ensuring the consequences for those that didn't, like Mr. Powell and Mrs. Abernathy.

But the most important thing he did was secure the dark web channels on which Vortex's little massacre was streaming. That and getting the word out to the right viewership. Thanks to the collection of wealthy sickos and sadists Wesley gathered, the event was netting him over one hundred million in profit. So far.

The event was pay by the hour, and with things slowing down, a few viewers had already dropped off. There was also a growing restlessness in the chat room.

G0reH0und: This is gettin' boring.

Rabbit7: The one with the jocks getting slaughtered in the cabin was better.

BeastHouse: That red-haired girl got one hell of a rump.

Belphegor: This shit better pick up soon or I'm out.

"Looks like we're losing the crowd, Wesley," Vortex said, a sinister smile spreading across his face as he looked at the file folders spread on his desk. They each had a label with a name written neatly across.

Ox.

Bull.

Fox.

Badger.

JAMES KAINE

"Time to feed the animals."

CHAPTER 12

L ogan stood in front of Kasey, tensed and ready to attack. The back of his neck was wet from the blood that had slowed but still seeped from the open gash on his head.

Kasey huddled behind him, hand on his shoulder. She grabbed a metal bowl off the shelf, the only thing that looked like it could have any type of impact if swung. They should have hidden in the hardware section.

"We know you're there, and we're armed. Show yourself!" Logan ordered.

Kasey looked down at the bowl in her hand and thought armed was a considerable oversell, but she supposed "come on out because we have no weapons" would give them less of a fighting chance.

"I ain't armed, and I don't mean you folks no harm," a male voice, deep and weathered, came from around the corner.

"Come out!" Logan barked, not softening his affect despite the third party's assertion he had no ill intent. "Slowly!"

A man limped around the corner with his hands raised and palms out. He was an older black man. Kasey would have guessed him in his sixties. He was bald, but what he lacked in hair on his head was made up for with a

133

bushy white beard. He was stocky with a bit of a gut but still looked solid and, even as an older gentleman, didn't look like somebody you would want to mess with. A prominent scar ran down the left side of his face, starting at the base of his temple and extending down to the middle of his cheek. The clothes he wore were simple, comprising a plain, gray, long-sleeve t-shirt and black jeans and gray sneakers. They looked brand new, as if he just grabbed them off a rack.

"I mean it. I'm not looking for trouble."

"Everyone here is looking for trouble," Logan said. "You don't want to cave our heads in for the chance at five million bucks?"

"Five million? Is that what's going on out there?"

"You don't know?" Kasey asked.

"All I know is there's a lot of noise and a lot of screaming coming from the concourse. I've been holed up in here the past few days."

"Few days?" Logan asked. "If you're not part of Vortex's game, what are you doing here?"

"I don't know who the hell Vortex is, but that's the name the people setting this place up the past few weeks been throwing around."

Kasey saw Logan's posture loosen a bit, but he still looked ready to pounce if the stranger made a wrong move.

"If you're not part of the game, what the hell are you doing here?"

"You hurt, son?" the man asked, sidestepping the question and slowly lowering one hand enough to point to the blood on Logan's neck. "There's a first aid kit in the office. Let's go talk in there."

"Why should we trust you?" Kasey asked.

"I dunno. Maybe you don't have to. But I ain't armed, and neither are you. Unless you think you're gonna knock me out with that fruit bowl there?"

Kasey looked down at the bowl in her hands and felt pretty dumb, but she didn't put it back. "Maybe," she said, not sure how else to respond.

"Your boyfriend there's a Marine. And outside of the wound, he looks to be in top shape. I think he'd do just fine against a broke-down old man like myself in hand-to-hand combat."

Her instinct was to correct him on the boyfriend comment, but that wasn't really important. Logan did need to get that head wound closed up. He didn't seem like he had a concussion, but Kasey wasn't a doctor so she couldn't be sure. But losing blood like that couldn't be sustainable if they were to get out of there.

She squeezed his bicep to signal to him that maybe they should listen. Logan released more tension and nodded.

"Ok, old timer. Lead the way."

The man led them straight to a small office in the back. Kasey recognized the layout as similar to Schow's. There were a couple desks, some older-style monitors that were off, and a timecard holder next to an old-school punch clock.

"Have a seat where you want," the man said, waving toward the desks.

Logan took a seat while still holding the towel to the back of his head, while the man opened a drawer in the opposite corner of the room and produced a medical kit.

"What's your name?" Kasey asked.

"Darnell. Darnell Banks," he said. "Want to let me fix up that gash for you?" he asked Logan.

"You served?"

"Yes, sir," Darnell said. "U.S. Army. Honorably discharged after a nasty battle where I ended up with this limp and a slightly less-handsome face." He pointed at his scar as he explained. "How about you?"

"Afghanistan. Honorable discharge. Going on almost two years now."

Darnell moved over toward Logan, still holding his hands out, one with the med kit, to show he wasn't looking for a fight.

Kasey didn't feel like she could trust anyone after what she saw on the concourse. Even Logan, who had gone out of his way to protect her, was still a stranger to her, even if she did feel some type of connection with him. She didn't feel that way with Darnell, but he carried himself in the same manner as Logan, clearly because of their shared military background. No, she didn't trust anyone, but these two men were her only allies at the moment. She wouldn't be able to escape on her own.

For a small med kit, it was stocked surprisingly well with supplies, including sutures. Kasey wondered if it had been planted specifically for the game.

She supposed the same question could be asked of their new companion.

"This ain't gonna feel great, my friend," Darnell told Logan as he held up the suture with the pre-threaded needle, "but I'm sure you've had worse."

Logan nodded as Darnell stepped behind him and poured some antiseptic on the wound. Despite that, he winced as the older man pierced his skin to start closing the gash.

"If you're not part of this fucked-up game, what are you doing here?" Kasey asked.

"I live here," Darnell said.

She wasn't sure she heard him right. "You live here?"

"I was chief custodian of this mall for fifteen years. When it went under a year and a half ago, I had trouble finding work. Couldn't make rent, so I got evicted. Made my way here and found out the keys still worked. Been holed up ever since. That was four months ago."

"If this place has been closed for eighteen months, why does it look like all these stores are still in business?" Logan asked. "Wouldn't they have liquidated their inventory before shutting down?"

"They did," Darnell replied. "This place was picked clean. I wasn't looking for supplies when I came here, just four walls and a roof. That was until two months ago."

"What happened two months ago?" Kasey asked.

"These folks started showing up and cleaning up the place, did all kinds of repairs and stocked the stores. By the start of November, this place looked like it never closed."

"Why would they go through all this trouble if they're just going to blow the place up?"

"It's a movie set," Logan stated as Darnell finished stitching him up and cut the suture. "This Vortex asshole is a streamer. He's obviously broadcasting this bloodbath, and this mall is the set. Whatever sick fucks he's got paying to watch this want to see a real working mall."

Kasey went quiet. It all made sense, in the most fucked-up way possible.

Darnell was focused on something else. "Can we not gloss over that thing you said about blowing the place up?"

"The guy who put this thing together says there're bombs set to level the building at two a.m. Have you seen anything like that?" Logan hoped Darnell had some type of affirmative answer.

"No, but I've been sticking mainly to the maintenance tunnels since they started working here. Only pop out occasionally to go get food or snag myself some new threads." He pulled on his shirt to emphasize.

"Maintenance tunnel?" Logan said, lighting up. "Does it lead out of here?"

"Yeah. That's how I been getting in and out without them finding me."

Now it was Kasey's turn to light up. "Where is it? Is it close?"

"Other side of the mall," Darnell said. By his expression, he knew that revelation would not be well received.

"Fuck!" Kasey shouted as she kicked the desk. Her outburst surprised the two military men. "We gotta go back out there?"

Logan looked down at his watch. "Unless you want to be blown to bits in about an hour and ten minutes, we don't really have a choice." He stood and turned to Darnell. "Let's gear up."

As if on cue, a siren blared throughout the mall. Kasey

knew that whatever it was signaling would not be good.

CHAPTER 13

"Whitney!" Eléna called at the bottom of the stairs. When she didn't get a response after a few seconds, she called down again. "Whit! Do you hear me?"

What the hell?

"She's probably on the other side of the store," Jim said, trying to be reassuring. "I'm sure she's okay."

"Well, if someone had stayed with her like we agreed, I wouldn't have to wonder," Eléna said, while her eyes burned a hole through Rachel, her voice coated with venom.

Scarlett was testing the grip on a baseball bat, her third. She didn't seem like any of them were to her liking. Eléna wondered if she was more concerned about how they matched her outfit than how hard they could hit someone.

"She's a big girl, sweetie," Rachel said. "I'm sure she wasn't all that thrilled to be with me, either."

This wannabe model was infuriating. Eléna wasn't normally the confrontational type, but she would love nothing more than to walk over and smack the smugness right off her painted face. Her self-centeredness and irresponsibility may have put her roommate in danger.

Just as she was about to announce she was going to look for Whitney, a siren pierced the silence that had fallen over the mall. It was like an air-raid siren from an old war movie. Given what happened over the past hour, it likely wasn't good and only increased her urgency to find her friend.

"I'm going up there," she announced, more to Jim than Rachel.

"Want me to go with you?" Jim asked.

"Go ahead," Rachel scoffed.

"No. Stay with her. She may actually need someone with her if things go down. I'll find Whit and we'll stick together."

"Ok," Jim said. "Be careful."

Eléna grabbed a baseball bat in one hand and a flashlight she found behind the counter in the other, then ascended the stairs. The interior of the store was dark, but there was enough light from the brightly lit concourse combined with the flashlight that she could find her way around.

The downstairs section contained most of the sporting goods—baseball, football, basketball, and soccer. Even with everything going on, seeing the soccer balls lined up on the shelves made Eléna sad. Her soccer career was over, and if she wasn't extremely careful, her life could be too.

When she reached the upper level, it was quiet. And empty.

The second floor was where most of the outdoor equipment was kept. Fishing poles, tackle boxes, and lures were off to the right. Straight ahead was hunting gear. Eléna didn't want to leave New Jersey, but at that moment she would have been grateful to be back home in Texas because their hunting sections had guns, something that would definitely come in handy. But

Jersey had very strict gun laws, so her aluminum bat was the best she could do at that moment. She saw bows and arrows on one display. She couldn't shoot a bow for shit, having tried when they did archery in gym class back in high school. But maybe Jim or Scarlett could. Not that she had much faith in Rachel being useful. Once she found Whitney, they would each grab one.

She heard a thump behind her and turned, shining her light toward the noise. She couldn't immediately make out the source, but there was camping equipment in that section, including a few tents that had been set up for a display.

Stepping carefully, Eléna headed for the display, shining her light in all directions to make sure no one could sneak up on her. She heard another sound as she got closer. This one sounded like someone stepping on something squishy. She looked down at her feet just to make sure she hadn't stepped in anything...unpleasant. The tile below was clean. Another squishing noise emanated from somewhere in front of her.

"Whitney?" she whispered. "Is that you?"

When she didn't receive a reply, she continued forward. Her light shined on one tent made of a darker material. As far as she could tell, there was no one there. She moved the beam to the one next to it, this one a cream-colored material. When it hit the tent, several large black splotches could be seen from the inside. Another squish followed.

What the hell?

She didn't want to look inside. Every part of her screamed to hurry back downstairs and get the hell out of the store. But what if it was Whitney in there? What if she was hurt?

Eléna steeled herself and took a deep breath. She lightly but quickly moved to the front of the tent. When she got to the flap, the obscene squelching sounds got louder. There was definitely something in there. She tightened her grip on the bat and pulled it back, ready to bring it down on anything inside that wasn't her friend.

She lifted the flap and saw Whitney. Or, more accurately, what was left of her.

Her roommate lay sprawled on the floor of the tent. From the inside, Eléna could see the black splotches were actually red from the blood that stained every corner of the canopy. Whitney's midsection was completely ripped open, her stomach a gaping cavern that revealed everything inside. The girl's face was turned to the side. Blood from internal injuries splattered her lips, cheeks, and chin as she no doubt coughed it up during her attack. Her tongue hung out of her mouth, and her eyes were wide, frozen in the final terrifying moments before she died.

A large hand scooped a handful of intestines and pulled it from Whitney's eviscerated torso. Eléna watched as the hand traveled to the man's mouth. He wore a black leather mask. The front face was stitched crudely to the cowl, and holes looked to be haphazardly cut around the eyes, nose, and mouth, giving it an almost jack-o'-lantern-like appearance. Leather buckles wrapped around the back, tying the obscene visage of death together.

The man shoved the guts into his mouth and took a bite, pulling a chunk of the innards away with a gush of blood as he ripped it open. He chewed and slurped it into his mouth like an oversized piece of spaghetti.

Eléna was grateful she didn't scream, but she couldn't

take credit for her restraint. She was petrified and couldn't will herself to move or talk. That wasn't enough to keep her from drawing the man's attention, however, because her flashlight beam shined right on him.

The large man's eyes bulged, and a demented smile creased his face at the sight of the fresh meat in front of him. His mouth was caked with blood and chunks of flesh. The gore slid down his neck and onto his hairy chest, which was crisscrossed with two studded leather straps. He was built like a strongman. His chest and arms were huge but not very defined. A prominent gut bulged from under the straps across his sternum. The maniac's teeth were crooked and yellow. He licked his lips, and Eléna could see his tongue was covered with leaking pustules. He grunted as he got to his feet, although the tent didn't provide enough room for him to stand up all the way.

Eléna stepped back as the man approached. He wasn't rushing, and as she regained her senses through her abject terror, she tried not to make a sudden move.

As he stepped out of the tent and stood upright, she saw just how big he was. He must have been close to seven-feet tall. His upper body was bare except for the straps. He wore a pair of tattered black pants and a pair of heavy-looking steel-toed black boots. The man was a horrifying behemoth that wore her friend's blood like war paint. He cocked his head at Eléna and smiled.

A bolt of ice pierced her spine, and every muscle in her body seemed to tense at once.

The man took his eyes off Eléna just long enough to reach back inside the tent. When he pulled his hand back out, it held the largest knife she had ever seen. It looked like a butcher's knife, but it was the size of a broadsword.

The blade looked very sharp, and there were serrated ridges in no discernible pattern along the length. It was covered in blood, both old and fresh, the latter of which dripped down over the man's hand and onto the floor.

Eléna unconsciously lowered the flashlight beam and illuminated what was left of Whitney. That was going to be her if she didn't get away from the psycho behemoth. So she did the only thing she could. She ran.

Fortunately for Eléna, she was far enough in her recovery that she could run forward, but her ACL was still delicate enough that any sharp turns could tear it again. If that happened, she was fucked. Another stroke of luck was the monster pursuing her didn't seem to be in a hurry, walking calmly and steadily while his prey ran for her life.

She made it to the stairs and slowed just enough to control her change in direction. She took a second to get her footing as she descended the steps, holding the side for support.

"Jim! Rachel! Get the gates open!"

When she got to the bottom, she turned and immediately saw Rachel holding her bat out in front of her, with Jim crumpled face down on the floor below, his glasses cracked and crooked on the ground next to him.

"What the fuck?" Eléna screamed.

"He was going to rape me!" Rachel yelled back.

"Fuck! We gotta get out of here!" Eléna shouted as she ran over to Jim and shook him, trying to rouse him.

"What are you doing? Where's your friend?"

"Shut the fuck up and open the gate!" Eléna ordered.

"What?" Rachel looked confused.

"Open the fucking gate!" Eléna really needed Rachel to keep up with what was happening. Eléna didn't look behind her, but she saw Rachel glimpse something in that direction. The look on Rachel's face told Eléna what she saw scared the shit out of her, because she immediately ran to the gate controls and hit the button.

Nothing happened.

She mashed it again and again, but the gate didn't respond.

Eléna turned and saw the beastly man standing at the bottom of the steps. He wasn't moving toward them yet. He was just standing there, his massive chest heaving as he regarded the trio of potential victims.

"Fucking motherfucking piece of shit," Rachel yelled desperately as she continued to pound on the button.

As she did, Jim was coming to. He groggily stood, with Eléna's help, while trying to compose himself. When he saw Rachel, he seemed to snap out of his daze as his face turned red and his eyes burned with anger.

"I wasn't going to fucking touch you!" he shouted. "I'm gay, you fucking moron!"

In the pantheon of famous last words, "I'm gay, you fucking moron" probably wouldn't have been Jim's preference, but they would have to do, because while his mouth was still open as he finished chastising Rachel, the giant's mammoth knife burst through the front of it, bisecting Jim's tongue, which parted like the Red Sea on either side of the blade. Jim's eyes looked like they were going to pop out of his head as blood poured from every orifice.

Eléna backed against the inoperative gate, next to Rachel, and they both screamed as the assailant yanked the weapon upward, splitting the top of Jim's face and head open with a sickening crunch.

The beast dropped his knife and stepped up behind

the man who was dead but had not yet fallen. He placed a hand on either side of his victim's bisected skull. He pulled both sides apart and wrenched them down until they snapped on either side of the jaw line, hanging like hinges to either side as a fountain of blood spurted from the bottom of his jaw, which no longer had a top.

Jim's body stumbled around a few steps but finally dropped to the floor with a nauseating splat.

The masked man smiled again as he turned to retrieve his knife.

Eléna knew the gate wasn't an option. She grabbed Rachel, who looked like she was trapped in some type of invisible box as she couldn't take her eyes off Jim's massacred body. Eléna's grip was enough to compel her out of her daze as Eléna pulled her toward the large window with the Lee's logo backward from their vantage point. She swung her bat hard and shattered the window.

Rachel didn't wait for the invitation and jumped out first. Eléna stepped up to climb after her but couldn't help herself from looking back at the man who was still standing, watching her. That sickening smile was still plastered all over his face.

Even if Eléna made it out of there alive, that smile would haunt her for the rest of her life.

CHAPTER 14

"What the fuck was that?" Dom asked.

"Sounded like a siren," Steve replied.

They had been reviewing the monitors, looking for a way out, when the piercing wail echoed throughout the mall. It reminded Steve of something you would hear in a war movie.

"No shit, Sherlock," Dom said. "What the fuck does it mean?"

"How am I supposed to know? I'm here with you. Why don't you email Vortex and ask him?"

"Not helpful, Steve-O," Dom said through gritted teeth.

"Let's see," Steve said, ignoring Dom's irritation as he reviewed the monitors. There were still pockets of contestants fighting throughout the concourse, but the spirited attacks from the beginning of the melee had died down to sluggish combat from injured fighters. Steve's eyes were drawn to a group of three men trading punches in a circle like they were part of some kind of fight club.

Out of nowhere, a chainsaw swung from somewhere off screen and sliced through the head of the man on the bottom right, sending it tumbling forward as blood spurted from the stump of his neck.

The sudden assault was enough to freeze the other fighters. They turned to run, but a small, skinny man jumped in like a bullfrog and landed on the back of one while using what looked like a scythe to slice the back of the other's ankles. While the small man then used his blade to chop at his prone victim, a larger figure stepped into the frame at the bottom. His back was to the camera, but Steve saw him raise the chainsaw and carve the other man.

"Who the fuck are they?" Dom asked.

"The siren must have been a signal for them to jump in."

Steve's attention turned to another camera, where a woman in a blood-stained pink shirt that read Be Kind was hiding behind a phone-repair kiosk. She didn't see another woman sneak up on her. The second woman wore tattered clothes, and her scarred face was covered at the top with black greasepaint. On her right hand was a metal apparatus with four long, sharp blades. The woman in pink didn't even notice until the other pulled her head back and shoved her knived fingers into her mouth, the blades popping out of the back of the woman's neck as the crazy woman cackled in amusement.

"Christ," Steve muttered. He had seen some nasty shit in his career, and some even worse shit tonight, but those new participants were displaying a gleeful sadism that put everything else he had ever experienced to shame.

He watched as the animals finished obliterating their prey before walking off in search of fresh blood. It seemed they were moving in the opposite direction of the security room. He was grateful for that, but he wondered how many psychopaths Vortex unleashed on them.

"Holy fuck!" Dom said excitedly as he grabbed Steve's shoulder and shook it.

"What?"

"There she is! There's Scarlett!"

Steve turned his attention to the monitor Dom was pointing at and saw that it was, indeed, the red-headed model climbing through the broken window of a sporting goods store. One of the college girls jumped out behind her. They ran away from the store, looking like they were being chased.

"Steve! You gotta go get them and bring them back here!"

"Are you out of your fucking mind?"

"Think about it. If we have some numbers, that'll give us a better chance of getting out of here."

"They ain't fighters, Dom. You're just thinking with your dick."

"So what if I am? Vortex will let up to five of us out. I'm sure Scarlett will be grateful to me for helping her out. Maybe that younger chick will show the same gratitude to you."

"You *are* out of your fucking mind. You want them, you go get them."

Dom's face twisted. He was pissed.

"Hey, *you* work for *me*. Or have you forgotten?"

"I haven't forgotten," Steve said as he turned back to the monitors. "I just don't give a fuck anymore."

That was a mistake, because the next thing Steve heard was the sound of the hammer on a revolver cocking back. He felt the cold steel of the barrel against his head a moment later.

"Just because I'm working with you for the time being don't mean you still don't owe us fifty grand. You know you can't walk out of here without that money. You also can't walk out of here without me, because if I die, Jimmy and Georgie will tell my pop it was you. Then it don't matter how much money you have, he'll find you and he'll kill you. So all this will be for nothing."

"Dom," Steve said, trying to sound calm, "this is foolish."

"We been here for like twenty minutes now. There ain't no exit we can see from the monitors, so we may as well get some numbers behind us so we can get out of here. You want to get one of these dumb dudes to join us? Who might backstab us and try to take us out? If you bring them girls back and they try something, me and you can take them."

Dom was an idiot, but he wasn't totally wrong, even though the reasoning he gave was total bullshit.

Steve had done a bunch of bad shit in his life, but he never thought of himself as a bad person, not completely. He couldn't see a way to sneak out of there, meaning they probably had to see Vortex's game through to the end. That meant only five of them could walk out. With him and Dom taking part in a tenuous team up, there was still room for three more. There was no reason those innocent girls should die if they could help it.

Plus, they needed to find a way out of there, because it was under an hour before the place would explode. Ideally, Steve would like someone out there to watch his back, but Dom was more of a liability. It was better he go at it alone.

"Fine," he said, "I'll go. So put the fucking gun down."

Dom smiled as he lowered the gun and carefully returned the hammer to its neutral position.

"I knew you'd see it was a good idea if you just thought

about it, Steve-O."

Steve didn't bother arguing with him. It was pointless. He looked around for some type of radio or way to communicate, but there wasn't anything obvious they could use.

"Listen, Dom," he said, trying to get the kid to be serious, "we can't afford any mistakes here. You'll be able to see me, but you won't have any way to communicate. If you see I'm in trouble, you may have to come after me. Do I have your word that you'll do that?"

"Yeah, Steve," Dom said, dropping the nickname in an attempt at sincerity. "I got your back."

Steve knew better than to believe him, but he didn't have any other choice.

"I'll be back."

CHAPTER 15

With his wound taken care of, Logan and Kasey followed Darnell to the hardware section. There were a ton of options to choose from. Logan strapped on a tool belt and loaded it with two hatchets, two hammers, a screwdriver, and a utility knife. With those in place, he selected a full-size ax to serve as his primary weapon. He thought about a chainsaw, but there was no gas, and even if there was, he didn't want to take a chance of it jamming or not starting on him.

Kasey also chose a hatchet and a hammer, opting for smaller, easier-to-manage tools, while Darnell also loaded up a tool belt similarly to Logan. For his main weapon of choice, he selected a nail gun. It was pneumatic, so it didn't need to be plugged in, but it needed to be attached to an air compressor. Darnell found a small portable version and plugged it in, letting it charge while the crew worked on gathering supplies.

While they were waiting on it to charge, Darnell produced a crumpled, soft pack of cigarettes. He bounced one halfway out of the pack and gripped it in his mouth to remove it the rest of the way. He held the pack out to Logan and Kasey, but they both politely declined. Logan had never seen the appeal of cigarettes, but he guessed Darnell was from that older generation that used to smoke everywhere.

Darnell returned the pack to his pocket and pulled out a Zippo, flicking it open and using it to light the smoke. As he snapped it shut, Logan got a good look at the emblem.

It depicted a grinning skull wearing a netted green army helmet. Instead of the usual portrayal of skulls with sunken, hollow, black eye sockets, this one had human eyes that bulged with a manic expression. It reminded him of the poster of one of his favorite movies from when he was a kid—*Evil Dead 2*. The inscription was two words, one above the skull and one below. It said Fuck Saddam.

"You've had that lighter a long time, huh?" Logan asked.

"Got it in '91," Darnell confirmed. He took a long pull on his cigarette and exhaled a plume of smoke that danced through the air and rose toward the halogen lights, where it dissipated. "It's my lucky lighter."

"This is going to sound ruder than I mean it to," Kasey said, "but it doesn't seem to be giving you a lot of luck at the moment."

"Sure it is."

"How?" she asked. "We're trapped in a mall that you've been living in since you lost your job and your apartment, may I add, with a bunch of bloodthirsty psychopaths in a game organized by a madman."

Darnell laughed. It was hearty and genuine. "Well, when you put it like that, it does sound bad." He took another drag. "But I'm alive. I also ran into the only two people in this madhouse that don't seem to want to kill anyone. And now we have weapons and a way out. I'd say that's lucky, wouldn't you?"

Kasey looked at Logan and gave him a shrug that said

he's got a point.

"I don't believe in luck," Logan said, "but if it helps us get out of here, I'll keep an open mind."

"Then that puts you ahead of most people in this world," Darnell said. He put the cigarette between his lips and checked the charge on the compressor. "Sixty percent. That'll do." He connected the portable compressor to the nail gun and took one last drag of his cigarette before dropping it on the ground and stamping it out with his foot. "Let's do this."

The trio, armed and ready for war, navigated the aisles to make their way to the front of the store. Logan felt better with weapons, but who knew how many people were left out there or if they had procured weapons for themselves. He got the sense not a lot of the people who had been brought in tonight were natural killers. They were just desperate folks put in an insane scenario. He was ready to use his ax on anyone who threatened them, but he hoped he wouldn't have to.

There was also the matter of that siren. Nothing apparent had happened since it went off, but who the hell knew what was waiting for them out there? It didn't take long for them to find out.

As they rounded the corner toward the entrance to the store, which was still blocked by the gate, they saw two men on the other side.

The first was big and jacked to all hell. He looked like Arnold in his prime. Logan clocked him at about six-feet tall, but his frame was pure muscle. He could see that through the cut-off flannel shirt he wore. It hung open, his arms, torso, and stomach exposed, revealing deep veins that ran along his muscles. He had a long, wild, black beard, and his hair was trimmed into a short

155

mohawk, like Animal from *Road Warriors*. His septum was pierced, and a large silver ring hung from his nose, giving him a bull-like appearance.

He held a large chainsaw that sputtered in his hands, waiting to cut through whatever stood in the man's path. The blade had already done some work tonight as it was smeared with fresh blood and chunks of gore.

His companion was a smaller man, probably no taller than five-foot-six. He was skinny and wore a leather vest and pants, with a spiked collar around his neck. His long, narrow face was clean-shaven but caked with dirt and blood. His grin was wide and unsettling, like the craziest versions of The Joker. Long, stringy, dark hair hung in front of his face, falling in front of his dark, devilish eyes.

He was crouched like an animal ready to strike. His arms were outstretched, each gripping a bloody hand-held scythe.

Logan felt Kasey press against him, having stepped toward him instinctively. He looked at Darnell, who was staring at the threatening figures on the other side of the gate.

"You seen these guys before?" Logan asked.

Darnell shook his head slowly. "This is a new one for me," he said.

"What do we do?" Kasey asked, trying to sound strong but her voice wavering.

"It's okay," Darnell said. "They're out there, and we're in here. Without a key, the only way to open the gate is from the inside."

As if on cue to mock them, the gate started to rise on its own. The grins on the faces of the bloodthirsty animals on the other side widened as their prey became exposed.

Fuck! Logan thought to himself, although the expletive

wasn't going to help them, so he shouted an order, giving the best strategy they had at the moment.

"Run!"

CHAPTER 16

I t looked like the coast was clear, but Eléna couldn't be sure. She and Rachel were hiding behind the fountain, the crystal blue water completely red as three bodies lay face down in the shallow water. Eléna peeked over the side to make sure the other two maniacs had moved on.

When they first escaped the sporting goods store, they had made their way back to the concourse. There were three men fighting, but they were quickly dispatched by a big man with a chainsaw and a smaller man with two curved knives. The trio was spread out twenty feet away from the girls' hiding spot. It was hard to tell who was who, as various body parts were jumbled together in a makeshift stream of gore.

"Are they gone?" Rachel asked, remaining in cover.

"I think so."

Rachel accepted the confirmation and stuck her head out from behind the fountain, seeing the coast appeared clear.

"Where do we go?" she asked.

Eléna looked around and pointed to an alcove. "There," she said. "Maybe there's a way out, or at least some supplies or weapons or something." She looked up to the second level but didn't see any signs of the giant who had killed and eaten her roommate. "Come on."

She carefully stood, with Rachel behind her. She was still furious with the woman, but at that moment, she was the only ally Eléna had. All hints of arrogance were gone since they escaped Lee's. There was nothing like witnessing brutal murders to make you humble, she supposed. But, more than that, Rachel was probably like anyone who made mistakes in life. You hid behind a persona you created because being the real you was too painful.

Eléna knew that all too well. Her pain started as physical with the two knee injuries, but the past week, since learning she was going to have to leave her dream school, she had had some dark thoughts. It felt like her life was over, and that made her desperate. So desperate that she dove headfirst into this shady-ass contest without knowing what it was actually about.

So, yeah, Eléna had made mistakes too—mistakes that got her roommate killed. Something told her she would need some serious therapy if she got out of there alive. But that was the key. She *wanted* to get out of there alive. She would go home to Texas and hug her parents and her brothers. Once she rested up, she would look at other schools closer to home, even if she had to do a year or two at a community college while she saved up to go somewhere to get her bachelor's degree. She would work two or three jobs, if that was what it took.

They eased into the darkened alcove, taking care to watch their step. It didn't matter. Eléna stepped on an otherwise innocuous tile, and it snapped under her foot. Before she could register what was happening, something gripped her foot tightly and she felt blood rush to her head as a rope broke through the tiles and up the wall. As the rope pulled her up, she felt the

JAMES KAINE

all-too-familiar pop as her ACL tore again, the second on this side and third overall. She couldn't help but scream as the pain exploded in her leg. She dropped her bat, which clattered to the floor.

"Shit!" Rachel screamed as she tried to prevent Eléna from being upended, but it happened too fast and the rope was too strong to stop it. Eléna cried as she hung helplessly while Rachel tried in vain to pull her down.

"I can't get you down," Rachel said in a panic.

Eléna had to fight through a mix of pain, fear, and sadness because she didn't have faith Rachel could get her down without her help. She strained to look up at the rope that was looped firmly around her ankle. It was threaded through a hole in the ceiling with no apparent source. She looked back down and followed a trail of broken tiles to the wall, but the mechanism of the trap was obviously behind the wall or ceiling and inaccessible.

"We need something to cut me down," Eléna told Rachel through heaving breaths.

"What?"

"I don't know!" Eléna said, getting desperate despite her attempts to stay calm. "Find something!"

"Fuck!" Rachel screamed. "Hold on!"

I'm not going anywhere, Eléna thought.

Rachel stepped around Eléna, to the back. She couldn't see in that direction, but she heard Rachel gasp suddenly.

"What?" Eléna asked. When she got no reply, she asked again, louder this time. "What??"

Rachel walked slowly back around Eléna's side. It reminded her of how she had stepped away from the large man in the sporting goods store. When she saw the red-head's face, she looked terrified.

"What the fuck, Rachel?" she said, trying to spin herself around to get a look at whatever her companion was looking at, but she couldn't.

Rachel's eyes welled with tears, and her lips shook. Eléna felt a wave of terrified panic as she understood what the woman was about to do. Her expression pleaded not to do it before the words came out of her mouth.

"Please, Rachel. Please don't leave me."

"I'm sorry."

Eléna probably believed her, but that didn't make things better, feeling that emptiness that had become too familiar to her as she watched Rachel turn and run away. She lost her scholarship. She lost her chance to go to Princeton. She was going to lose it all.

She felt somebody behind her even before she saw the metal claws snake around the back of her head and to the front of her face.

"Please! Don't!" she screamed, pleading with the person behind her.

The pleas fell on deaf ears as she felt the metal press against her face, one finger against her forehead, another directly over her eye, one across the bridge of her nose, and the last one across her lips and chin. She winced and cried as she felt them dig in, and she screamed as white, fiery agony slashed her face along with the claws.

A burning pain shot through her forehead. Her left eye went blind as the blade sliced the orb open. She felt the cartilage splinter as another ripped through her nose, and when she instinctively brought her tongue to her upper lip, a huge chunk of it was torn away, exposing her teeth and gums. Her entire face quickly became a mask of wet crimson.

She heard a high-pitched laugh as her attacker stepped around her. The woman was wearing ragged clothes, and her scarred face was painted black on the upper half. Her claw apparatus was attached to one hand, and she held a long, serrated knife in her other. The animal cocked her head as she regarded Eléna, like an artist admiring her work.

Eléna had already spoken her last words. There was no point in using any more. The only thing she could do was scream as loudly as she could through the blood pooled in her mouth. She only hoped someone would find her and stop this maniac before she ended her life.

The trapped girl's shirt hung down, bunched around her neck, and exposed her stomach. The evil woman smiled as she ran her clawed index finger down the length of it, not cutting, just brushing along the flesh. Eléna braced herself to be stabbed, but to her surprise, the woman pulled her claws away and crouched so they were eye to eye. She placed her knife on the tile and cupped the back of Eléna's neck with her unarmed hand.

She pulled Eléna in and planted a kiss on her ruined lips. It was sloppy, more licking than kissing. Eléna screamed into the woman's mouth as she felt the psycho slide her tongue along the torn flaps of Eléna's upper lip. After a few moments of this indignity, the woman stopped and stood back up, a Cheshire-Cat grin spread across her bloody mouth. When she crouched down again, Eléna thought she was going to go for another gory kiss, but she grabbed her blade instead.

Eléna was so focused on the knife that it caught her off guard when the woman slammed her claws into Eléna's stomach. She wailed in inexplicable agony as the sadistic bitch turned her hand with the claws still embedded in her stomach, tearing the flesh and causing her internal organs to squeeze out like sausage coming out of its casing.

She continued to scream as the woman swung her knife into the side of Eléna's neck, sending a spray of blood onto the floor below. A second swing cut even deeper, more than a quarter of the way through.

It took several more hacks to remove Eléna's head, but mercifully, she died before the final strike.

CHAPTER 17

"Head for the office!" Logan shouted as the trio ran back into the store.

Kasey was keeping up, and so was Darnell, but he was concerned about the older man's limp. He didn't want to look back and risk slowing down, but the gate mechanism had stopped and he heard the revving of the chainsaw, which sounded way too close for comfort.

They ducked into an aisle in the toy section and came out the other side with a clear view of the hallway leading to the office where Darnell had patched him up not too long ago. Any notion of safety was quickly dispelled, however, when the smaller man leaped off the top of the shelves next to him and blocked their path, smiling as he ran his scythes together like a chef sharpening his knives before cooking.

"Damn it!" Logan yelled and turned, only to see the large bull with the chainsaw was approaching from the other end.

"What do we do?" Kasey asked in a panic.

Darnell answered with actions rather than words. He raised the nail gun and fired three in the small man's direction. He dodged them with almost-inhuman reflexes, ducking into the aisle and leaving an opening for them to move forward. Logan couldn't see the smaller

164

man anymore, but Darnell turned and fired two more nails into the aisle to push him farther back.

Logan grabbed the shelf to his right and toppled it, along with the packs of action figures that lined it. The large man with the chainsaw just laughed and cut through it to create a path. Logan kept knocking rows of shelves over as they moved to the office, hoping to at least slow the Leatherface wannabe.

When they reached the door, Kasey gripped the handle and barely moved her hand out of the way as a scythe flew end over end through the air, embedding itself in the door frame, right next to the knob. The smaller man leaped forward and crashed into Kasey, knocking her onto her back.

Darnell responded quickly, shooting a nail into the man's forehead. It staggered him, but it didn't penetrate far enough to do actual damage. The man responded by using his second scythe to slash at the older man's hand, slicing it and causing him to drop the nail gun.

Kasey used the distraction as an opportunity to grab one of her hatchets. She swung, but her attacker brought his blade up to block hers, the metal sparking as it clashed.

Logan felt the big man's shadow fall over him, and his battlefield instinct told him to drop, which he did just in time for the chainsaw to whoosh over his head. The attack took the man off balance, and Logan took advantage by kicking him in the shin. It did the trick as his attacker fell to one knee, giving Logan the opportunity to kick again, this time landing square on the man's nose, knocking him back and sending his chainsaw skittering down the aisle, the teeth cutting into the tile as it slid to a stop against one of the toppled bookcases.

His instinct was to go help Kasey, but he had to trust her and Darnell, because if this big bastard got back up and got his weapon, they would be fucked.

Logan raised his ax and charged the man, who was still shaking off the effects of the kicks. Unfortunately for the retired Marine, the bullish man recovered quickly and rolled out of the way as the ax bounced off the floor. Logan almost lost his grip but held on. The miss gave his opponent an opening, and as Logan raised it for another strike, he felt the man's meaty fist dig into his side. He felt his ribs crack as all the air left his lungs, failing to be replaced.

As Logan gasped, the man stood and grabbed him by the neck, whipping him with incredible strength into the wall, smacking the side of his head into the sheetrock. Logan swung wildly, peppering the man with ineffective body blows that the behemoth simply laughed off as he tossed Logan back, sending him sliding across the floor.

Logan was battered, but he knew he couldn't take too long to compose himself because he saw the bull stand and walk in the opposite direction to retrieve his chainsaw. He rolled on his stomach and pushed himself up.

Darnell was down, holding his right hand with his left as blood seeped through the fingers.

Kasey and the smaller of the psychopaths were nowhere to be seen.

"Darnell!" Logan shouted. "Snap out of it! Get Kasey."

The old soldier shook it off and looked to see what Logan had seen. Kasey was gone. He looked back to Logan, who simply said, "Go!" He stood and ran off as Logan rolled to his right, just narrowly avoiding the chainsaw as its wielder swung it downward.

It was Logan's turn to take advantage of the man's failed attack. He reached for the first weapon he could get out of his toolbelt, gripping the handle of a screwdriver. Pulling it from its sheath, he drove it into the top of his opponent's foot, eliciting an anguished, guttural cry as it went in. The man held on to his chainsaw and flailed it in Logan's direction. Logan was barely able to duck—a precise swing would have ended him, but he managed to dodge it. He reached down to his toolbelt again and came out with a hatchet. Logan didn't hesitate to drive it into the man's thigh, cutting through his pants and embedding it deep in his muscled flesh.

The psychopath reached down in an attempt to remove the ax while taking another one-handed swing with the chainsaw. Logan was ready, however, having grabbed the other hatchet. He sliced the man's massive bicep as the colossus tried to bring his weapon forward. The chainsaw fell to the ground as the man's torn muscles prevented him from keeping his grip on it.

Logan pounced on his enemy, slamming the hatchet down on whatever body part was the closest. Rivulets of blood poured down the man's body as Logan's hatchet took chunks of flesh off his chiseled physique. Surprisingly, the giant remained on his knees, weathering the assault even as his limbs failed him.

Logan took a step back and saw the man hunched over on his knees, too many gashes in his flesh to count. The goliath heaved labored breaths, but he did not fall. Once the Marine's assault ceased, the man looked up and smiled as blood poured from his mouth, soaking his beard. A sound started from deep in his throat. It was a guttural chuckle that morphed into a full-blown maniacal laugh.

Logan looked at his hatchet but saw something better on the ground. He dropped the small ax and replaced it with the chainsaw. As he raised it up, the man continued to laugh. He laughed and laughed and laughed, right up to the point where Logan cut off his head.

He actually took out Bull, Vortex thought to himself as he watched the carnage unfold on his monitors.

When he started planning the game, he knew there was going to be a point where the contestants stopped fighting each other and started trying to work together to get out. That was where The Animals would come in. He had recruited—or captured, depending on how you wanted to look at it—this "family" of psychopaths a few months back. After some promises of plenty of fresh meat to play with, they agreed to play along, although negotiations weren't their forte. When the contestants decided to form alliances, that's when beasts would ensure the carnage continued.

At least the audience was responding well, based on the comments. They loved watching Bull and Badger take out the three men fighting on the concourse, but what Fox had done to the Mendoza girl was chef's kiss! Fox was the unofficial leader of the group. The guys were just sadistic brutes. Not that Fox wasn't a sadist herself, she just had a little more brain power than the rest. She was the one that convinced the others to work with them, which was why Vortex gave her a little more leeway to roam outside, taking care of Dominic Capelli's goons.

Where the hell is Ox? he thought. Fox was the brains, but Ox was the attraction. He was possibly the biggest man Vortex had ever seen, both in height and bulk. His evisceration of and, um, post-mortem activities with Mendoza's roommate were also well-received, but Vortex would like a little more out of him in the less than an hour this little production had left.

He could worry about that later. Talbot's defeat of Bull was unexpected, but Collins and the interloper still had Badger to deal with. He turned to the monitor to watch as the animal hunted.

Kasey found herself hiding back where she and Logan had started when they first took shelter there. The bloody dish towel and the metal fruit bowl were still on the floor in the middle of the aisle.

"Little pig, little pig," a scratchy male voice came from somewhere behind.

Kasey pressed herself against the shelves and covered her mouth with one hand as her breath quickened, trying desperately not to give away her position. In her free hand, she held her hatchet, her grip so tight her knuckles were turning white. She felt the sweat drip down the back of her neck over the fine hairs that stood on end.

For a long moment, the store went incredibly silent, to the point Kasey wondered if she had lost her hearing.

She hadn't, because suddenly, she heard that same raspy voice. Only this time, it was above her.

"Come out, come out," the man called Badger hissed as Kasey looked up in time to see him drop from the top of the shelves and land square on her, knocking both the wind out of her and the hatchet from her hands. He only had one of his scythes, but it was raised and ready to strike.

On pure instinct, Kasey reached for the nearest object, which turned out to be the metal fruit bowl she had ineffectively threatened Darnell with just a short time ago. The stainless steel felt cold in her grip as she swung it, hitting Badger across the cheek and diverting his blow as the blade ripped through the pile of towels on the shelf.

"Bitch!" he yelled as he rubbed his cheek.

She swung again, hitting him in the temple and knocking him off her.

I guess it is a decent weapon, she couldn't help but think as she crawled back to get to her feet.

Unfortunately, Badger did a kip up, jumping from his back to his feet with ninja-like reflexes. He pulled his scythe from the pile of towels and immediately charged at Kasey, bellowing like the wounded animal he was.

Kasey raised the bowl, unconvinced it would work again.

As she prepared to swing, Badger's pace became jerky, as if he was hit by something from behind. He halted and turned. As he did, Kasey could see past him, where Darnell stood at the end of the aisle, holding his injured hand against the formerly fresh t-shirt stained with blood and his other holding the nail gun. She could see three large nails protruding from her attacker's back.

Badger charged Darnell, who pulled the trigger on the nail gun only to find it was empty.

Kasey, seeing her hatchet at her feet, grabbed it and chucked it in Badger's direction without thinking. She felt her breath catch in her throat as she realized if she missed, it could hit Darnell instead.

That wasn't the case. The ax landed between Badger's shoulder blades and sent his entire body into a spasm as he fell forward, dropping his weapon and stumbling toward Darnell. The nail gun was empty, but it wasn't useless as Darnell swung it in an uppercut motion, sending Badger off his feet and onto his back, his head striking the ground hard.

The maniac was dazed but not dead, which meant he was still a threat. He rolled onto his stomach and tried to reach back to remove the hatchet from his back. Kasey, moving again on pure instinct, rushed forward and helped him by yanking it out, a gush of blood coming with it. The injured man rolled onto his back with an agonized scream and looked as if he was trying to kip up again.

Kasey didn't let him. She drove the ax into the middle of his face, splitting his nose as the blade sunk into his skull. He emitted an indescribable scream of agony as Kasey pulled the hatchet out and chopped his face into a bloody mess of chopped meat. She screamed as the ax rose and fell again and again and again as she unleashed years of anger on this man who tried to kill her—anger for her husband being taken from her, vitriol for her sister being such a stuck-up fucking bitch, rage at some pissant fucking YouTube guy who caused the death of so many innocent people that night.

Such was Kasey's blind rage that she was unaware of her surroundings until she felt a firm grip on her wrist preventing another strike with the hatchet, while another arm wrapped around her waist, pulling her back. She struggled to get free, turning herself. She fought until she realized it was Logan who held her.

He let her go when he saw she realized it was him. As she stared at his blood-splattered face, she saw a mix of worry and relief in his eyes. As long as it took that amount of rage to build within her, it left just as quickly. Tremors shook her face as the second part of her catharsis overtook her and the sobs started. She reached out and threw her arms around Logan and pulled him in tight. He winced but didn't pull away as he hugged her back, holding her while she cried.

Amid the emotional moment, she had momentarily forgotten about Darnell, until she heard him speak.

"God damn, Kasey, you killed the shit out of that motherfucker!"

CHAPTER 18

Rachel ran away from the girl she had left to die as fast as she could. The guilt was suffocating. But what the hell else was she supposed to do? She had no way to cut her down, and if she stayed, they both would have been killed.

Was she the last one left? There was no sign of anyone else alive. Piles of mutilated corpses littered the concourse, which was covered in more blood than every horror movie she had ever seen combined.

She approached the area where they had started and looked toward the exit. The ill-fated man who tried to run out before the game started lay in front of the doors, his brains trailing away from him, following the trajectory of the sniper's bullet. Maybe enough people were dead she could just walk out and claim the prize. There couldn't be much longer before the place blew up. Could she chance it?

As she contemplated it, she heard heavy, stumbling footsteps from her left. She saw a large man in a biker outfit staggering toward her. His arms were outstretched like a zombie, and blood poured from two ruined eye sockets.

"Where the fuck are you?" the man said in a deep, pained voice. "I can fucking hear you!"

She was ready to run toward the door when she felt someone grab her from the other side. It was an older man, looking to be in his fifties. Everything about him screamed cop to her, but that didn't mean she could trust him.

"You Scarlett?" he asked.

The question shocked her. She had wanted to be recognized when she first got there, but her career wasn't necessarily her main priority anymore.

"Uh, yeah," she answered without thinking. *Oh fuck, is this guy going to force himself on me?*

"Let's get you to safety," he said.

"Why should I trust you?"

Before he could answer, the blind biker lunged forward with an, "I'll fucking kill you!" The cop pulled a revolver and shot the man in the chest, hitting him in the upper left quadrant, just off the shoulder, and sending him crashing to the ground.

"You got a choice?" he asked her.

She supposed she didn't.

On the way to the security room, the man told her his name was Steve and he was, in fact, a police detective. He said he was with another man who had made it to safety, and they were planning to get out of there. They had seen her and Eléna on the monitors and wanted to help them both but, unfortunately, were too late to save Eléna.

As she stepped into the security room, she thought she would feel safe, but something about the whole thing raised her hackles. The other guy was some Jersey Shore wannabe who looked at her like she was a meal and he hadn't eaten in weeks.

"Scarlett! Thank God my friend Steve found you!" he said, sounding like the type of kid who over-emoted his way through every theater audition.

She looked at Steve, who seemed as disinterested in her as his buddy was enthusiastic.

"Uh, yeah. Thanks for helping me," she said, choosing her words carefully.

"Of course!" the man said. "My name's Dom. I hope you don't mind me saying, but I'm a *big* fan!"

That explained it. She guessed playing into her persona was a smart move, because it just might have got her out of there. Rachel put her Scarlett Saint mask back on and gave Dom her best seductive look as she held out her hand. He eagerly accepted it and planted a kiss on top of it.

"Well, if you get me out of here alive, I'd say you earned a free subscription."

The guy looked disappointed at that. He was expecting more. Of course he was.

"We gotta get out of here first," Steve said, looking at his watch. "We only got about forty-five minutes to figure this out."

"We just gotta see who's still alive," Dom said, like it was the simplest thing in the world. "If it's just the three of us, we can walk out of here and split the money."

"You think he's actually going to pay us?" Steve asked.

"Why not? We played by the rules and we lasted."

Rachel stepped closer to Dom and ran her fingers down his chest, playing the game. "You'd really split the money with me?" she asked.

Dom put his hand around her waist and pulled her close. She could practically see the drool forming in the corners of his mouth.

"Absolutely. Assuming you're nice to me."

CHAPTER 19

L ogan would have liked nothing more than to hold Kasey until she was ready to move, but time was not on their side.

"We gotta go," he said. "We'll get to that maintenance tunnel and get you home to your boy."

The mention of her son was strategic. He knew that would spur her on to move, even if she just wanted to stay put and cry. She broke the hug and looked up at him, blood and tears streaking her features. He put his hands gently on either side of her face and assured her. "I'll get you home."

They cautiously made their way toward the other end of the mall. Bull and Badger were dead, but they didn't know if Vortex had unleashed any other maniacs for them to deal with. They checked in all directions as they continued their trek, ready to attack if attacked.

"I don't know about you, son," Darnell said, "But, even on my worst days in Iraq, I ain't seen nothing like this. You?"

Logan thought about it before answering. "On my last tour, my chopper was shot down over the Helmand Province in Afghanistan. My squad was mostly killed, all except my best friend, Alex. We fought our way out of there, but I'll never forget the carnage I saw that day."

"Worse than this?" Kasey asked.

"No," Logan replied. "We signed up to fight. We knew we were putting our lives on the line. Have I seen bodies mangled and fucked up beyond recognition like we have today? Yes. But these are all ordinary people that were forced to commit unthinkable acts of violence against their neighbors. And for what? Money? Fucking YouTube views? I've seen some senseless violence, but this takes the damn cake."

The trio fell silent. Darnell reached into his pocket and retrieved his cigarettes and lucky lighter. He lit the smoke, but before he could return the lighter, Logan whispered a command.

"Get down!"

They ducked behind a kiosk. Logan craned his neck around to confirm he saw what he thought he did.

The body of a headless woman hung from a rope tied around one leg and affixed to the ceiling. Her shirt was bunched around her neck, and her stomach was torn open. Her intestines hung down and draped over her stump. The head was on the floor, lying in a pool of blood to the side. It was facing Logan and his friends. The features were indistinguishable as it had been sliced to shreds by what looked like claws.

As if the entire scene wasn't disturbing enough, another woman was lying underneath the corpse. She was very much alive and letting the blood flow over her. One hand was splayed out to her side, an apparatus with four sharp claws affixed to it. Her other hand was thrust inside her pants, rubbing her crotch as she writhed in pleasure, a large machete-esque blade lying at her side. Logan could hear her moan, and when her mouth opened, she eagerly lapped up the blood that dripped into it.

The bar for the most horrendous fucking thing Logan had ever seen was getting raised by the minute.

"I don't think she saw us," he said to Darnell, who was huddled next to Logan, with Kasey behind him. "We need to move, but do it *quietly*." He pointed to another kiosk about twenty yards ahead. "We'll go one at a time."

Logan stayed low and moved out from behind the kiosk. Keeping his eyes on the distracted, crazy woman, he moved quietly and quickly, managing to duck behind the kiosk without drawing her attention. Kasey moved next, mimicking Logan's movements as she made it to the new hiding spot without incident.

It was Darnell's turn. He wasn't as fast as Logan, but as long as he was quiet, he should be okay. He returned his lighter to his pocket, but in his haste, he must not have pushed it down far enough, because Logan saw the lighter fall out of Darnell's pocket, hitting the tile with a clink as he lunged forward to move toward his companions. It was a good thing Logan didn't believe in superstition, because Darnell dropping his lucky lighter would have been a bad sign if so.

Darnell had almost joined them when the old soldier froze as the tile he stepped on sank down.

Logan heard the click. He knew what it was but couldn't react fast enough.

Darnell's eyes met his, and Logan saw the fear a split second before the landmine went off.

Darnell exploded in a haze of red mist. The tile must have been rigged as a pressure plate to trigger the mine. The blast shot up directly under him as his body flew apart in all directions, adding to the piles of gore spread throughout the mall.

The explosion had consequences beyond killing their ally. He was close enough that Logan and Kasey were knocked back by the concussive force of the blast, which sent them and the kiosk crashing to the ground.

Logan tried to compose himself, but between the ringing in his ears and the pain wracking his body, it was no simple task. He looked at Kasey. She was also writhing on the ground but looked otherwise intact. He called her name but couldn't hear the sound of his own voice.

Pushing himself up, he turned to a seated position and saw blood blossomed in all directions, along with chunks of meat from the man that used to be Darnell Banks. His lucky lighter lay amidst the gore that covered the area. It was as if whatever good fortune he had vanished the second the lighter was removed from his person. No, Logan Talbot wasn't superstitious, but at times like that, he understood why people were.

To his right, in a pile of Darnell's innards, rested the lighter, somehow intact and hurled in that direction by the blast. He couldn't say why but, even in his dazed, injured state, he didn't want the only thing left of the man's legacy to be buried in the mall when it became a pile of rubble, so he pocketed it before turning his attention back to his still-living companion.

"Kasey!" he called again. This time he could hear himself as the ringing faded.

"Lo...Logan," she said weakly as she tried to get herself up onto her elbows. "What happened?"

"Darnell's...gone. We gotta move."

That was an understatement. In the chaos of Darnell's explosive goodbye, Logan had forgotten all about the maniac pleasuring herself under the headless corpse. He looked back in that direction and saw the woman was standing, her claws and a knife at her side. She laughed as she watched the horrid scene in front of her.

Logan got to his feet and put his arms under Kasey's shoulders, helping her stand too. She was dazed, so he shook her.

"Kasey! We gotta get the hell out of here! Now!"

CHAPTER 20

"Jesus Christ!" Rachel heard Steve shout as the explosion rocked the security room, shaking the floors like an earthquake. "What the hell was that?"

Before anyone could answer, the security room went dark. Both the lights and the monitors went out, and darkness enveloped the room. Rachel screamed despite trying to hold it in. Every time she thought she had the rules of this messed-up game figured out, the puppet master threw in a new wrinkle. Who knew what the hell was coming for them next?

While she hoped someone had a lighter or some kind of light source, the room lit up again, this time awash in a red hue. The monitors remained dead.

"Security lights," Steve said before she or Dom could ask the question.

"What about the monitors?" Dom asked. "They gonna go back on?"

"Doesn't look like it."

"That was an explosion, right?" Rachel asked in panic. "What time is it? Are we too late?"

Steve looked at his watch. "It's 1:21 a.m. We still got about forty minutes."

"Fuck!" Dom shouted. "We gotta get the fuck out of here, right fucking now, Steve."

"I agree," Steve said, "but if we walk out without being sure that there's less than five of us left, those snipers are going to take our heads off."

"Then you need to go check."

Steve looked more than exasperated. Rachel was surprised he didn't protest. Dom was younger, but Steve was bigger and looked a whole hell of a lot tougher. But the older man acted pretty subservient toward the younger.

"Fine," Steve said before turning to Rachel and giving her an odd look. "You going to be okay staying back here while I scope things out?"

"She'll be fine," Dom answered before she could.

Steve held her gaze. Something in it told her she needed to be very careful about how she interacted with Dom. But with that psycho lady with the finger knives and that big son of a bitch with the gimp mask roaming around, she would rather take her chances with DJ Pauly D over there.

Rachel nodded.

Steve focused back on Dom. "If I'm not back by 1:45, just make a run for it. Better to chance the snipers than get blown up."

It was Dom's turn to nod. Steve left the room, and Rachel was alone with Dom. He took a deep breath and turned around, putting both his hands on his head, looking severely stressed out.

It was at that point she saw the gun tucked in the back waistband of his pants. She tensed, realizing she was in just as much danger in here as she would have been out there.

Dom turned back and glued his eyes to her as a lecherous grin spread across his face.

"I really am a big fan," he said. "You do superb work."

In her mind, Rachel sat down and let Scarlett stand up. She was the one that was going to get them out of there. They were almost out of time. There were maniacs roaming the mall with weapons, and everything she incorrectly thought about poor Jim was embodied in Dom. She needed to get out of that room and out of that mall. She would take her chances with the snipers.

"Thank you," she said, taking on the low, sultry voice of her online alter ego. "What's your favorite thing I do?"

"Sheesh," Dom said. Rachel wondered if he knew how ridiculous he sounded. "I love it all, but you give incredible blowjobs."

"Mmm," she said, taking a step toward him. "You ever wonder what it would be like to be on the receiving end of one of those?" She licked her lips to punctuate the question.

"Of course. I always picture myself in the guy's place."

She took another step, standing right in front of him. She raised a perfectly manicured finger to his chest and ran it in a zig-zag motion down to his stomach, stopping just short of his crotch. Leaning in, she cupped the back of his neck and pressed her lips up to his ear.

"You get me out of here alive, and you won't have to picture it," she said before giving his lobe a light nibble. "You'll experience it live." She felt Dom's body tense up and took this as an opportunity to slide her hand down his back. "I'll even let you cum on my face, if that's what you want."

"Yeah, baby?" Dom said. "You'd be that nice to me?"

"Oh yeah," she said, practically moaning as she reached the small of his back, not wanting to move too suddenly to risk giving her actual intent away. "If you help me, I'll let you do *anything* you want. *Nothing* off limits."

"That sounds..." He trailed off suddenly.

She had to make her move, so she quickly grabbed for the gun, only to find it wasn't where she thought it was. The barrel was pressed against her forehead.

"Sounds like you think I'm fucking stupid," Dom said as he pushed her away from him.

Fuck!

"I'm sorry," she said as panic set in; she put her hands up in surrender. "I would just feel more comfortable if I had the gun, but I didn't think you'd just give it to me. Really! I wasn't going to hurt you! I just wanted to feel safe, you know? We can still do all those things I said. I want to! I swear!"

"Oh, really?" Dom asked.

"Yes!" she replied desperately.

"You know who my father is?"

Rachel shook her head. "N...No. I'm sorry, I don't."

"My pop is Carmine Capelli. He's what you civilians would call a mob boss. In our family, loyalty means everything, so I know those that are loyal and those that aren't. And you, sweetheart, you ain't got a loyal bone in your body!"

He cocked the hammer back, and Rachel let out a frightened whimper, not wanting to jar him into shooting her with a full-blown scream. She was terrified, and while the threat to her life was her primary concern, this gangster asshole actually cut her deep with that last statement. She had never been loyal to anyone in her life. Her parents, her ex-fiancé, Jim, Whitney, and Eléna had all suffered the consequences of her betrayals, costing them relationships, hopes, dreams, and even their lives. Rachel had only ever thought about herself.

The consequences of her selfishness had chipped away at her psyche, her health, and her self-respect. It looked like it was finally going to cost her everything she had left.

"Take off your clothes," he ordered.

"What?" she asked.

He stepped forward and pressed the barrel directly between her eyes so hard it stung. "Take off. Your. Fucking. Clothes."

"Okay! Okay!" Rachel stripped off her shirt and tossed it onto a bank of monitors.

"I'm a reasonable guy. It's not the first impression you make with me, it's the last. You want to be loyal?"

"Yes!" Rachel said as she wiggled out of her tight leather pants.

"Then you're going to prove your loyalty right now."

"I...I don't think we have time..."

"We got enough," Dom said, the look on his face absolutely psychotic. "And, the way I see it, if we *are* about to die, I'm not going out without getting the Scarlett Saint experience!"

She stood before him in just her underwear. She had been naked on camera too many times to count, often filming her most intimate of moments, but for the first time she could remember, she truly felt exposed, standing in front of the crazy gangster.

"Lose the bra and get over here," he said, motioning to her with the gun in one hand. His other lowered the zipper on his pants.

Rachel did as he said, unclasping the bra and letting it fall in front of her as he leered at her.

"Yeah! They look even better in person!" He motioned again with the gun, and she stepped forward as he dropped his pants and underwear before pulling out his decidedly less-than-impressive manhood. "Time to show some loyalty."

Rachel took a deep breath and got to her knees without further instruction. She let Scarlett take the lead and got to work on his member. It was just another indignity in a life full of them. Rachel Dubois didn't want to be here anymore than she wanted to have fucked all those people on camera. None of it had done anything for her. It didn't give her satisfaction in life. It didn't give her the money she thought she would make. Hell, she rarely even had an orgasm, so what the fuck was any of it for?

At that moment, she was doing it to save her life. Yeah, it had been a shitshow, but maybe she could turn it around.

She reached around and grabbed Dom's buttocks, encouraging him to thrust. Time was not on her side, and if she was going to have any chance at all, she needed to get him off quickly. Her efforts appeared to be working as the young mobster moaned obscenely.

"Fuck yeah!" he grunted. "You like that, don't you, you little slut?"

She moaned an affirmative as she added her hand to his shaft, trying to speed it along even further.

Rachel Dubois made a silent plea. She didn't believe in God, but if there was a higher power out there, she promised that if she could somehow survive, she would quit porn and go home. She would do everything in her power to repair her relationship with her parents, money be damned. Even if it meant taking an office job, she would do it. Or retail. Or waitressing. She would gladly dive into any of those professions she used to look down on as beneath her. She finally got it. It didn't have to be too late for her.

But it was.

She was so busy working Dom—and he was too busy enjoying it—that she didn't hear the door behind her open.

The last thing Rachel felt was a sudden burst of pain at the top of her head. The blow that killed her came from a very large knife that split her cranium down to the space between her eyes. There were ten seconds between the impact and the end of her life, ten seconds of horror that her damaged brain witnessed before it shut down.

Ten...

Unfortunately for Dom, one of Rachel's last motions was the spasm that clamped her jaw shut, severing his most prized possession.

Nine...

Dom screamed and fell backward against the table behind him as blood spurted from his crotch, looking like a mannequin whose lower body was painted red.

Eight...

Dom raised the gun through his panic and pain, firing off a shot.

Seven...

Ox, the large man from the hardware store, lunged forward and grabbed Dom.

Six...

Ox slammed Dom's head into the metal table, caving in a portion of it at the temple.

Five...

The mammoth maniac slammed Dom's head again, sending his eyeball popping out. It landed next to Rachel's right knee.

Four...

Ox yanked his massive knife from Rachel's skull.

Three...

He slammed the knife through Dom's neck, severing his head.

Two...

Ox raised the head, the stump of the severed spinal cord jutting from the bloody stump as blood poured onto the floor. He held it in front of Rachel as if he knew she could still see it.

One...

The world went black as Rachel died.

CHAPTER 21

Logan was hurting. Every step was filled with pain as he limped away from the scene of the explosion that killed Darnell. He had to think there were more landmines hidden beneath the tiles, but he had no way to detect them and couldn't afford to take his time as the crazy woman gave chase. To make matters worse, the power had gone out temporarily before the backup lights came on, but they were dim and red, making it hard to see.

Kasey was doing her best to pull her weight, but she was hurt too. She was also a civilian, so she had no training in a combat situation, including pushing through the pain to finish the mission. The woman had fought more than admirably tonight, but she had her limits and she was there. Logan held her arm over his shoulder and did his best to support her while they moved forward.

The psycho woman, Fox, was taking her time in pursuit. Logan knew he and Kasey weren't anywhere near top speed, but she was clearly toying with them, sauntering after them at barely above-normal walking speed.

"C'mon, Kasey!" Logan said, offering a battlefield pep talk. "Let's move it, soldier!"

"I'm...trying," she said through the pain.

And she was. She picked up the pace, and they started moving faster.

Logan stole a glance back and saw Fox had picked up her pace but still didn't appear to be in any great hurry.

They kept moving, reaching the concourse, where most of the initial action took place and which was still littered with bodies of the contestants, many of whom had spent Thanksgiving dinner with their families only a few hours earlier.

As they passed the fountain, a large figure lunged toward them. Logan saw the man, who was slow enough that, even in their injured state, Logan managed to stop short and let him crash to the ground.

They stepped around Otto, the blind biker, quickly and continued to move forward. Logan stole another glance back and saw the burly man struggle back to his feet.

Otto's eyes were gone, courtesy of Logan, but he had suffered other injuries, too, including what looked like a broken nose and a bullet wound in his chest. Yet, somehow, this guy was still moving forward like a bulldozer without a driver.

As the biker moved forward, Fox stepped around him. For a moment, Logan thought she would ignore him. Instead, she thrust her clawed hand up through the bottom of his chin, a guttural wail sounding throughout the concourse. It quickly became a gurgle as she twisted her hand, slicing through his gums and tongue, scraping the roof of his mouth as she curled her fingers to grip the jawbone from the inside. She never took her eyes off Logan as she mutilated the man, capping her assault off with an inhuman display of strength as she detached his lower jaw from the rest of his head.

The man stumbled around almost comically, in a

slapstick kind of way, his tongue, now split in two, dangling from the vacant area where his jaw used to be. He took two steps to his right before tripping over the side of the fountain and falling in facedown, where he remained, finally off the board for good.

Fox cackled as she broke into a run, ready to give Logan and Kasey the same, if not worse, treatment.

There was an alcove about thirty yards ahead with a sign above that read Security and Maintenance, with arrows pointing toward it. That had to be where the tunnel access was located.

Logan picked up his own pace, and Kasey did the same, but they couldn't move as fast as the woman who was rapidly closing ground.

We're not going to make it, Logan thought as he prepared himself to fight.

Just as he was ready to let go of Kasey and turn to fight the psychopathic woman, a man stepped out from the alcove. It was the cop Logan had seen when they first got there, the one that was buddied up to the mobster. He had a gun, and it was aimed right at them.

It was over. A crooked cop with a gun stood in front of him, and a madwoman with a large blade and Freddy Krueger finger knives was behind them. Even if by some miracle he could fight them both off, they had maybe thirty minutes, tops, before the place blew up.

The report of the pistol rang throughout the concourse, and Logan shut his eyes tightly, expecting to die.

A second later, he opened them and saw the man standing in front of them, gun smoking, but the bullet hadn't hit Logan. He turned back and saw Fox down on one knee, holding her side as blood sluiced through her fingers. Murderous rage burned in her eyes, and she got to her feet, lunging forward before another bullet hit her just above the right breast. She tried to step forward, and the cop fired again, hitting her in the left shoulder. The last shot was the one that dropped her.

"Fuck!" the man shouted. "I didn't want to have to use that many bullets."

"Assuming you didn't use anymore, you have three left. You going to use them on us?" Logan asked, not having the time or patience for any more games.

"Depends," the man said. "You going to try to take me out?"

"We just want to get out of here," Kasey said.

"Well, by my count, there's three of us here. I got two...companions in the security room. Math was never my thing, but it seems like we're the final five."

"You think Vortex is going to just let us walk out of here?" Logan asked.

The man chuckled. "No. But what choice do we have?"

"What if I told you there was a way out? A way that took us out past the snipers?"

"I'm all ears, buddy." Steve cocked his head and raised an eyebrow in feigned interest.

"The people in the security room—who are they?"

"Just people like you and me."

"Can they be trusted?" Logan had a good idea who at least one of those people was, and he didn't like it.

The man laughed again, louder this time. "Who the fuck can we trust?"

He had a point. Logan looked at his watch—1:38 a.m., twenty-two minutes until the grand finale. "Let's get to your companions. We'll tell you then."

CHAPTER 22

A night of unimaginable atrocities still didn't prepare the trio for what they saw when they walked into the security room.

Dominic Capelli's head was on the floor in a pool of blood. The left side of it was caved in, and the eye socket on that side was vacant. His eyeball wasn't far away, lying in a pool of unidentifiable fluids. The young mafioso's face was frozen in an expression of abject terror and unimaginable pain. His body was crumpled next to it, pants down around his ankles and a bloody hole where his penis should have been.

To his side was a twisted hunk of metal that looked like it used to be a .38-caliber revolver. If it was, it was useless.

The woman who had referred to herself as Scarlett lay on the table in the center of the room, almost completely naked. The top of her head was bisected down to the bridge of her nose, and pieces of bone and brain matter floated in the puddle of blood that pooled around her. There was a bloody chunk of something lodged in her mouth. Logan had a pretty good idea it was Dom's missing appendage. He couldn't fathom the scenario that had led to their deaths, not that he wanted to.

At the side of the table where the woman's ruined head lay, the one called Ox, the largest man Logan had ever seen, sat in a metal chair that buckled and threatened to collapse under his weight. His massive body was caked with blood. He reached into the gaping cavern of the dead woman's skull and pulled out a string of brain matter, popping it into his mouth, chewing the tough meat as blood dripped down his chin.

Ox stopped eating when he noticed the trio interrupting his dinner. He smiled, displaying his bloody, rotten teeth as he stood, his massive frame almost touching the ceiling.

"Run!" Logan shouted yet again as they exited the room, slamming the door shut behind them.

The maintenance room was at the end of the alcove, thirty yards away to the left. Before they could head that way, Kasey saw something to her right.

"Oh, shit!" she yelled.

Logan looked in that direction, and Fox was standing still, eyeing her prey and blocking off the end of the alcove, leaving them only one direction to go.

"Get to the maintenance room!" Logan yelled. "Hurry!"

As Logan headed that way, with Kasey by his side, he heard a bang followed by a searing pain in his upper right thigh. It caused him to lose his balance and buckle to the ground. He hit the floor and looked at the hole in his jeans, from which a generous amount of blood was seeping out.

Steve stood over him, smoking gun in hand. "Sorry, pal. Thanks for your service." With that, the crooked cop grabbed Kasey and dragged her toward the room.

"Get the fuck off me!" she shouted.

He put the gun to her head and said, "Not another word," as he continued to drag her toward the maintenance room.

Logan struggled to his feet as Kasey screamed his name, while Steve dragged her off. He looked in the other direction and saw Fox stalking toward him. If she was feeling the effects of her gunshot wounds, she wasn't showing it.

Adding to Logan's growing list of problems, the security room door burst open, almost coming completely off the hinges as Ox ducked into the alcove, carrying a massive knife that looked more like a sword. He still had chunks of Rachel's brains staining his chin, neck, and chest. He stepped toward Logan but stopped when he heard a high-pitched whistle.

"Minnnne," Fox said in a drawn-out, raspy hiss. "Get the others." She pointed toward the maintenance room as Steve ducked inside, pulling Kasey along with him. Ox ignored Logan and lumbered after them.

He wanted to give chase and help Kasey, but Fox wouldn't let that happen. He turned and squared up. She stepped into a fighting stance, drawing both arms back behind her, claws on her right and blade in her left as she crouched, ready to strike.

Logan initiated the attack. She was expecting him to remain on the defense, so the best way to counteract that was to go on offense. He let out a guttural battle cry as he put the pain out of his mind and lunged at the woman.

Fox was surprised, but she was able to sidestep his attempt at a spear. She spun around on his right side and slashed his back with her claws, tearing through his shirt and slicing into the flesh, splattering the wall with a gout of blood as it sent her opponent crashing to the ground. The pain was overwhelming, but Logan couldn't just lay down or he was dead.

He kicked his leg back, trying to take her down with a

leg sweep, but she jumped and responded by plunging her knife toward his chest. Logan caught her wrist and stopped it from piercing his heart. He used both hands to push her arm back. Although he could move it back, she was much stronger than she looked. And she had a weapon in the form of claws on the opposite hand. While Logan struggled to keep her knife out of his sternum, she slashed at him with the finger knives. He caught her other wrist just in time, but the blades were long enough that they scraped his face, drawing thin sheets of blood.

The woman grinned like the maniac she was as she craned her head down and licked the blood off his face. That gave Logan the opening he needed as he drove his forehead into the bridge of her nose, breaking the bone and sending her flying off of him with an angry cry of pain.

Logan struggled to his feet as she recovered. Just as he got his footing, she did a kip up move, not unlike Badger during the fight back at Keene's. As soon as she got to her feet, he put all his power behind a right cross that slammed right into her broken nose.

Her eyes watered, impairing her vision as she swung both her knife and claws wildly.

Logan ducked an especially uncontrolled slash and drove his shoulder into the woman's midsection, his second attempt at a spear successful. As he drove her off her feet and carried her back into the security room, she plunged the claws into his upper back, right at the left shoulder blade. It took everything he had to fight through the pain of the slash on his back and the bullet in his leg to stay on his feet and drive her onto the table next to Rachel's mutilated body.

He delivered punches to her stomach and chest, trying

to hit her around the bullet wounds to maximize the pain. But no matter how much he inflicted, she still fought ferociously.

She slashed at him with her knife, and he ducked back, barely avoiding the blade as it whizzed past his jugular, missing it by a centimeter. She followed up with a claw swipe, and Logan sidestepped. Fox pivoted to continue her assault. Logan dodged another stabbing attempt, but the woman kept at it.

Less than an hour ago, Logan Talbot had told Darnell Banks he didn't believe in luck. Darnell respectfully disagreed, and moments after he dropped his lucky lighter, a landmine turned him into a fleshy jigsaw puzzle. If that sequence of events hadn't made Logan reconsider his belief in luck, what happened next did.

Fox stepped toward him, finger knives raised for a devastating strike, but she stepped on Dominic Capelli's eyeball as she did. The orb wasn't a match for the madwoman's boots, which easily flattened it, but the fluids that had already pooled, along with the release of what was left, were enough to cause her to slip and lose her footing. Her leg slid out from under her and she fell back, hitting her head on the edge of the table, dropping her knife on impact.

Logan didn't hesitate to grab it, turn it, and drive it straight into her chest. An explosion of blood spurted from her mouth as the blade found its home in her sternum, breaking through her breastbone and piercing her heart. Insane until the end, Fox laughed hysterically as she grabbed Logan's wrist and tried to pull her own knife out of her chest.

She swiped at him with her claws, but Logan again caught her wrist. Much of her strength was gone, and

Logan found it easier to manipulate her limb, turning the claws toward her and, using all the power he could muster, driving them into her throat, snapping her forearm in the process.

Fox stopped laughing and started coughing as her mouth and throat filled with blood. After a minute, she stopped moving, and the hand that wasn't embedded in her esophagus fell to her side. She was dead.

Every part of Logan's body hurt. He wanted nothing more than to collapse and take time to gather whatever strength he could. But that wasn't an option. His watch said 1:48 a.m. The mall was going to explode in twelve minutes. Plus, Kasey was still in danger, both from the crooked cop and the giant cannibal that was after them. He had to move.

Logan spit a blood-filled loogie next to Fox's dead body and got to his feet. He pulled the knife from her chest and headed for the maintenance room.

CHAPTER 23

"Get your goddamn hands off me, asshole!" Kasey yelled at Steve as he dragged her into the maintenance room. It was a sizeable area that reminded her of a warehouse. It was lined with shelves containing boxes of who knew what. She supposed this was where Vortex's guys kept the supplies and fake merchandise they used to stage the mall. There was also an apparatus with various pipes running from it and up through the ceiling. Kasey assumed it was the mall's HVAC system.

"Shut up!" Steve shot back, pointing the gun at her to emphasize he was the one in charge.

"Why do you need me?"

"I'm sorry, kid. Really. But we're gonna get out of here. We needed someone to slow down those psychos, and I figured better to sacrifice your boyfriend out there than you. I'm trying to show you a kindness."

"You're fucking sick," Kasey spat.

"Yeah, well, I got no compunctions about using you as bait, neither, so I'd watch my mouth if I were you." Steve gave her a look that said *I got no fucks to give, lady*.

She slapped him. It must have surprised him, because he loosened his grip on her, allowing her to run toward a row of shelves, looking for cover. She kept her head down, expecting to hear a shot ring out behind her, but one didn't come. Was he out of bullets?

It didn't matter. She didn't have time for questions. She had to find the entrance to the maintenance tunnels. Feeling the effects from the multiple injuries she obtained throughout the night, she limped around the shelves, past a row of lockers, and saw a clearing with a square hatch that had a handle on the floor. That must be it.

"Get back here!" she heard Steve shout from behind her.

Kasey reached the hatch and pulled the handle, but it didn't budge. She tried again with all her strength and it moved slightly, but it was so heavy she couldn't get it open. She was screwed.

To make matters worse, the maintenance room door flew open, and she saw Ox's giant frame enter the room on the other side. He wasn't looking in her direction, and she knew she couldn't open the hatch on her own, so she decided hiding was her only option. She moved as quietly as she could to the lockers and slipped inside one, taking care to close it quietly as the beast stalked his way through the room.

Through the grate, she saw Steve duck behind a row of shelves. He had his gun at the ready, but Kasey still didn't know if he had any bullets left. For a few moments, the room was silent save for the giant lunatic's footsteps as he stalked his prey.

Steve looked terrified as he huddled out of sight. Kasey didn't know what he was going to do, but the irony that he was the one providing the distraction while she hid wasn't lost on her. The footsteps stopped, and after a long, tense minute, she thought maybe Ox had left the room.

Unfortunately for Steve, that wasn't the case.

The shelf the police detective was hiding behind suddenly crashed on top of him, pinning him to the ground and sending his gun sliding across the floor. The behemoth that was Ox stood over the toppled rack as Steve tried to push the boxes off, some of which had ripped open in the fall, littering the vicinity with packing peanuts.

Ox bent over and gripped Steve on both sides of his head, using his immense strength to yank the man free from the metal shelf that pinned him. Kasey heard an audible crack as his spine snapped from the brutal, abrupt way he was pulled from underneath.

The monster's smile was clear under his mask as he lifted the helpless man off the ground, his useless legs dangling underneath him.

"Don't!" Steve pleaded. "Please..."

The monster had no compassion. Kasey saw the muscles in his forearms tense as he applied pressure to Steve's head, whose screams reached their apex before they faded, replaced by a sickening crunch as his skull started to give. The scream turned to a gurgle just before his head exploded in Ox's hands like the watermelons that old-school comedian used to hit with the mallet. Chunks of ruined cranium flew everywhere.

A piece of his scalp got enough distance to slam into the locker where Kasey hid. As it hit the grate, a spray of blood got through and splashed her face. Kasey brought her hand to her mouth to try not to scream.

She watched as Ox dropped the headless body back onto the toppled shelf. That evil smile crossed his face as he admired his work.

She prayed he wouldn't look in the lockers for her,

but he looked right in her direction. She didn't know if it was because he knew she was there or if he was just looking around, but it felt like her breath was trapped in her throat as her heart jackhammered like it was trying to escape her chest. She thought about just jumping out and trying to outrun him, but where was she going to go? The place was going to blow up in less than ten minutes. That hatch was her only option, and if she couldn't escape, she would rather be blown up than suffer whatever sadistic death this monster planned for her.

She felt relief when she saw him turn in the other direction. Was he leaving?

The respite was short-lived as Ox retrieved his weapon and turned back in Kasey's direction, heading directly for her. The behemoth stepped up to the locker and crouched down so he could look in through the grate.

When that twisted, evil smile again spread across his face, Kasey screamed.

CHAPTER 24

Logan burst into the maintenance room and immediately collapsed as his wounded leg gave out from under him. Kasey's terrified screams echoed through the large room, and he focused in that direction as he struggled to his feet.

From the entrance of the room up to the bank of lockers against the opposite wall was a path of destruction. Shelves and boxes were toppled, the contents spread over the floor, mostly Styrofoam packing material. On top of an overturned rack lay Steve's body, twisted in an unnatural angle and a smashed chunk of meat where his head used to be. Behind that stood Ox, the large man crouched down and peering into a locker while Kasey's screams filled the area. She must have been hiding inside.

The man didn't seem to notice him, being too focused on terrorizing Kasey, so Logan limped toward him, Fox's large knife in hand. He tried to be quick, knowing he likely only had a few moments to get to him before he ripped the door off and got to her.

When Ox reached for the door and grabbed the handle, Logan yelled to distract him from opening it. It worked, because the animal turned in time for Logan to drive the serrated blade into his gut. The big man let out an inhuman cry, more of anger than pain, as Logan twisted the knife between his ribs.

Ox grabbed Logan by the throat and immediately cut off his air supply. He lifted the Marine off the ground and brought him to eye level. Logan could smell the putrid stink of Ox's breath as he brought him in close. His dark eyes were filled with nothing but hatred and mania.

Thinking fast, he withdrew the knife from Ox's side and slashed it across his chest, severing the leather chest straps in the process as a large gash opened across the man's torso. Another angry yell escaped him, tossing Logan onto the felled shelves. He landed on Steve's massacred corpse, which cushioned his landing somewhat. But he lost the knife in the process.

Ox lunged at him with his own colossal blade, swinging it down hard.

Logan just barely managed to roll away as it cut through Steve's body like it was cookie dough. Logan didn't stop moving as he crawled over the shelves and back to the concrete floor. Every inch of him hurt, but his legs and back had the worst of it. He didn't know how much longer he could push before he passed out.

And he had to keep pushing, because the big man's assault was relentless. He lumbered toward him, and Logan tried to limp away. The man wasn't as fast as Fox or Badger, but he was fast enough, and Logan was moving forward on sheer will, which wasn't enough to create separation. It reminded him of when he would drop into man coverage from the linebacker position on the football field. Linebackers weren't usually as fast as the defensive backs, so it was key not to let them create distance or the assignment would be blown.

Ox raised his weapon over his head, and Logan sensed

it coming. He quickly grabbed the end of the closest shelf and pulled it down, smacking it into Ox and knocking the knife from his hand. The enraged beast of a man pushed the shelving off and rushed Logan, spearing him into the ground. It felt like someone dropped a shipping container on him.

Ox stood over his felled opponent and caught his breath. He only took a moment, though—the time for games was over.

Logan was dazed, but he still caught the look the monster gave him. It said this was it. Logan was a dead man.

Kasey had never been so scared in her life. Logan had somehow survived his encounter with the crazy woman and rushed in just in time to stop Ox from getting to her. But her savior was in trouble as the monstrous killer had gotten the better of him. Kasey couldn't just let him die. Looking at it selfishly, she understood that once he killed Logan, she was next, but it wasn't just that. She didn't want Logan to die, either. This entire night had been a maelstrom of violence, death, and betrayal, yet through it all, Logan had remained steadfast in protecting her. She wanted to do the same for him. How she would do it, she had no idea.

She exited the locker, trying her best to stay steady, the weight of her own injuries threatening to make her keel over at any moment. Logan was down on the ground to her right, Ox standing over him. He didn't have his knife—that was on the ground a few feet behind him. A bit behind that was Fox's knife. It was smaller, and from her hiding spot, she had seen Logan use it on the man with little impact. But that was maybe her best option.

She looked around for anything else she could use and saw something better. Steve's gun was near the shelves his massacred body rested on. Kasey remembered wondering if he had any bullets since he didn't shoot her when she ran away. Time to find out.

Kasey retrieved the revolver and aimed it in Ox's direction just as he leaned down to grab Logan. She fired. The bullet shot from the chamber and found its home in Ox's back, directly between his shoulder blades. She was aiming for his head, but it clearly wasn't high enough.

Worse than that, the impact diverted Ox's attention from Logan, but it didn't drop him. He turned toward Kasey, an enormous ball of rage. He stomped toward her, only stopping long enough to retrieve his blade.

Kasey pulled the trigger again, and the gun clicked empty. She pulled it three more times in rapid succession as panic set in. The large man loomed over her. She turned to run, but she didn't have anywhere to go. She tried to climb over the felled shelving, but it was too late. A flash of white-hot pain exploded in her abdomen as Ox's blade entered her back and burst through her stomach.

Logan got his senses just in time to see Ox stab Kasey. The beast drove his monstrous knife through her, then picked her up while she was skewered.

"No!" Logan screamed as he got another burst of adrenaline. He moved as fast as his injuries would let him and jumped on Ox's back, wrapping his bicep around the man's throat.

Ox dropped Kasey to the floor, hard, and withdrew his knife, sending a spray of blood with it. He flailed and tried to shake Logan off, but Logan held on with everything he had. He saw the bullet wound in Ox's back and drove two fingers of his free hand into it, eliciting the most inhuman sound from the big man yet. He hooked the fingers and pulled, ripping the flesh even farther as rivulets of blood dripped down the animal's massive back.

This sent Ox into a frenzy as he thrashed even harder. In that moment, it would have been more appropriate if he was the one called Bull as he tried to buck the smaller man off. It was only when Ox turned and drove his entire frame backward, slamming Logan into the lockers and denting them in, that the Marine lost his grip. He crumpled to the ground as the giant took a few steps forward and shook his head to compose himself.

When he had his bearings, he turned and roared, charging his felled opponent. Logan reached to his left to grab anything he could use to defend himself, and luck had his back again. He grabbed the handle of Ox's knife and got it into position just in time for the psycho to land on it as he lunged forward.

The blade pierced him in the center of his upper abdomen, and his eyes went wide in disbelieving shock as his own weapon impaled him. Despite the wound, he still reached out and grabbed Logan's neck.

Logan tried to twist the knife, but his strength had waned. As his breath left him, he thought about Alex and his family. He felt like he failed them, just like he failed Kasey. He didn't know the woman, not really, but they had bonded, and in just a few hours, he had grown to care about her as much as people in this situation could care about each other. But it wasn't enough. They were both going to die.

But he didn't die. Ox's grip suddenly loosened as the man coughed up a vile concoction of blood and bile that hit Logan in his face. Ox fell to the side, and Logan caught his breath.

Pushing the big man off him, he immediately ran to Kasey. The blade had torn through her midsection on the bottom left. She had lost a ton of blood, which pooled around her motionless body. Her skin was pale, and her lips were blue. He didn't see the rise and fall of her chest, but he got to his knees and put his fingers to her neck. She had a pulse, but it was very weak.

His watch said 1:57 a.m., three minutes until the place was due to go up. He saw the maintenance hatch and didn't hesitate to grab the handle. The thing was heavy. He would have had trouble lifting it even if he wasn't severely injured. But it did budge, and he fought as hard as he could to raise it. It took a Herculean effort, but he opened it.

209

Scrambling over to Kasey, he lifted her off the ground. He got her over his shoulder and descended the ladder into the tunnel.

The first thing he noticed as he got to the bottom was a strong smell of gas. He wasn't sure exactly why, but the only thing he could figure was the explosion that killed Darnell must have broken a main somewhere. Fortunately, the tunnel was illuminated by halogen lights; otherwise he would have no light source because Darnell's lighter would cause an explosion.

The path was lit, but only toward the end. He couldn't see any type of exit. It didn't matter. His only path was forward.

Keeping Kasey on his shoulders, he focused on taking one step after another. Every time he put weight on the leg Steve shot him in, it threatened to buckle and collapse, but he kept upright. Every step allowed him to see a little farther down the tunnel, but it revealed nothing other than more tunnel. There was still no exit.

He had gone about thirty yards when he heard an enormous thump behind him. He turned his head and saw Ox standing at the bottom of the ladder, his knife still jutting out of his stomach. This monster had taken everything Logan had to dish out, yet he was still coming for them.

Logan knew the only way he could outrun him was to drop Kasey. He wasn't going to do that. She wasn't dead yet, and even if it didn't look good, she had become a warrior tonight, a comrade-in-arms. He would not leave her behind.

As Ox started toward them, moving slowly and deliberately, Logan gently put Kasey down. Resigned to his fate, he sat against the wall of the tunnel and pulled her into his lap. He pressed his face against hers and listened to her shallow breaths. He kissed her forehead and said, "I'm sorry," as he reached into his pocket and took out Darnell Banks's lucky lighter.

Logan Talbot was prepared to die if it meant taking Ox with him, but an explosion from above rocked the tunnel before he could ignite the lighter. The entire place rattled and shook as debris fell from the ceiling. Logan stole a quick glance at his watch, which read exactly 2:00 a.m. Vortex wasn't bluffing.

More explosions could be heard from above, even drawing Ox's attention as he looked up. The mall had been built during the nineteen fifties, so tunnels like this were often used as bomb shelters. Logan was thankful for that, because it kept the area insulated from the blast which would have ignited the gas leaking into it.

One more large blast shook the area as Ox continued toward them. They had been spared the explosive death in the mall, but that still looked like the way they were going to go out. He touched his finger to the flint wheel, ready to send them all out in a blaze of glory.

Suddenly, a huge chunk of ceiling collapsed onto Ox. It drove the monstrous killer into the ground as more slabs of concrete broke off the ceiling and smashed into him, crushing him under the massive weight. Only Ox's arm was free. Logan could see the maniac slapping his hand against the ground, trying to claw in and pull himself out, but finally, it stopped and fell limp.

At last, Ox was dead.

It was just after 2:15 a.m. when Logan came out the other end of the tunnel. It led to a small satellite office in the wooded area outside the mall's perimeter. He figured it had been used for maintenance workers to get in and out of the tunnels underneath as needed, but it had long stopped being used for that purpose, even before the mall closed down.

It was being used as a home. A military-style cot was set up in the corner, and there was a small table with a stack of books, mostly self-help and advice on starting your own business. In one corner was a cooler and a bowl filled with various snacks, like bags of potato chips and TastyKakes. A picture of what looked like a much younger version of Darnell with a smiling woman and young girl rested by the bed.

Logan didn't have time to reminisce. He laid Kasey carefully on the bed and checked her pulse again. He couldn't find it. Putting his ear against her mouth, he didn't feel her breath.

No!

He started chest compressions, adding two breaths after every thirty pushes. He repeated it again and again but didn't get a response.

Logan had seen so much death in his life and faced it even after returning from war. His best friend was fighting a deadly illness, and over fifty innocent people had been killed in Vortex's game. He was losing this woman who had fought with him all night to survive.

"Kasey!" he cried. "Stay with me! Please fight!"

He kept at the hopeless task as the tears broke through, and for the first since he was a child, Logan Talbot cried.

CHAPTER 25

B rad Dockery, the man the world knew as Vortex, pulled his three-million-dollar Bugatti Chiron into the driveway of his Santa Cruz beach house. The luxurious domicile was a marvel of contemporary architecture, with large windows designed to maximize the ocean view and natural light.

He felt good as he stepped out of his car. It had been two weeks since the show at the mall, and it appeared all loose ends had been tied up.

There were no survivors, just as he had planned. Talbot and the Collins girl had escaped down a maintenance hatch. Brad had known about it and understood it was a potential exit route, but he hadn't seen a need to post anyone at the outlet in the woods. If someone had gotten in there, he would have plenty of time to send someone to head them off. Even if, by some miracle they got away, he had ample resources to find them, as Mr. Powell and Mrs. Abernathy found out before their untimely ends.

He had gotten a bit nervous when Talbot and Collins made it in there, but the bombs went off only a few minutes after. In the weeks since, neither had resurfaced, so he was confident they were buried in the rubble underneath the remnants of Oatbridge Mall.

Collins had surprised him. He knew Talbot would be

a formidable fighter, but he had assumed Collins would be easy fodder for the others. Not only had she held her own, but she and Talbot took out The Animals! That was a bonus, because it saved him the trouble of having to eliminate those psychopaths himself.

Add in an unexpected performance from Scarlett Saint, and his little production was a rousing success—a success to the tune of $186 million dollars in profit!

His backers were already requesting he plan his next show. He would have loved to do one for Christmas, but that was too soon. Wesley had paid off local authorities to let his crews handle the clean-up, and they were doing yeoman's work in getting rid of the bodies they dug from the rubble. As they found new corpses, they were transported to a funeral home owned by one of Brad's shell companies, where they were incinerated in the crematorium.

Sure, there was going to be an uptick in missing persons cases throughout New Jersey, but it wouldn't be long before they got lost in the shuffle. A big part of the reason he held the contest there was because the state was so densely populated.

The contestants' disappearances wouldn't go unnoticed, but it wouldn't be as obvious as more sparsely populated areas.

The best part was, since everything was broadcast on dark web channels, his more mainstream persona was intact. Vortex could go on streaming video games and posting prank videos, raking in cash from the idiot youth of America. The money he would make from the luxury condos he planned to build at the site of the old mall would be nice too.

It wasn't in his best interests to push through with

the next game so soon. He had spent more than a year planning the last one, and that diligence paid off. It would be easier next time, but it still wouldn't behoove him to rush. He had a great concept for Easter. If he started planning in the next week, he may be able to pull it off.

When he turned off the alarm and stepped into the house, the automatic lights didn't go on. What the fuck? All the money that shit cost, and it didn't even work half the time!

Irritated, Brad went to flip on the light switch. Before he could, he felt a pinch in his neck. He slapped at the area thinking he had been bitten by a bug, but his vision blurred and he passed out.

Brad woke up in his bed. That wasn't unusual. What was strange was he was lying on top of the comforter, buck naked. He also couldn't move anything below his neck. He felt panic set in as he lifted his head.

There was a camera set up at the foot of his bed and a laptop next to it. The screen displayed what the camera saw—Brad, naked and vulnerable, paralyzed on his bed. A patch was on his right hip. It looked like a large Band-Aid.

"What the fuck is going on?" he shouted.

"Pipe down, Brad." A man's voice came from his left.

He turned his head as far as he could in that direction and saw his Vortex helmet resting next to him on the pillow. He also saw Logan Talbot sitting in a chair next to the bed. The soldier's face still carried some bruising from the battle two weeks ago but looked to be healing.

He held a rocks glass filled with a rich, amber liquid in his hand. The crystal decanter on the end table told him it was the Old Rip Van Winkle 25-Year-Old bourbon he had purchased at an auction two years ago. There were only seven hundred and ten bottles ever produced, and he had spent almost $44,000 buying it.

Talbot took a sip of the liquor and put the glass down with an exaggerated "Ah!" He produced one of Brad's Arturo Fuente Opus X cigars. The box of twenty cost Brad $1,500.

The Marine took out a silver Zippo lighter emblazoned with a skull in an army helmet with the inscription Fuck Saddam. He used it to light the cigar, taking a puff and blowing a plume of smoke at Brad.

"What did you do to me?" Brad screamed.

Talbot picked up the glass, took another sip of the expensive liquor, and set the glass back down, next to the decanter.

"Brad, we don't have a lot of time here, so how about you let me do the talking?"

"What? How are you alive?" Brad couldn't believe Talbot had made it out.

"I'm a Marine, Brad. I've survived a lot of nasty shit. Your little contest at the mall may actually have been the worst. It almost did me in. But...I guess I'm starting to believe in luck." On the last part, he turned the lighter over in his hands, regarding it reverently.

"You see, Brad, I've been blessed to work with some

incredible Marines in my day. Some of them went on to careers in other government agencies, like the CIA. When you're tight with intelligence agents, some who even owe you their lives, that gives a person a lot of resources."

"I don't know what the fuck any of that means!" Brad blurted, earning a smack in the face for the outburst. He couldn't feel anything below his neck, but he felt that.

"You've got an extensive network," Talbot continued. "But you ain't shit compared to the United States government. My friends got me out of there and kept me hidden to give me a minute to recover while they put a dossier together on you. Well, they didn't put it together so much as pull the file they already had. When arrogant pricks like you live their whole lives online, it's very easy to put a file together on them.

"You think because you know some basic coding, you're anonymous? Uncle Sam always knows who you are. Most of the time, they'll leave you be. But when you kill fifty people for your sick pleasure, you'll end up at the top of their list." He puffed on his cigar.

"If I had died, you probably would have gotten away with it. But once I told my buddy in D.C. about your little game, I got you greenlit."

"What did you inject me with?" Brad knew he was screwed.

Talbot pulled an empty syringe from his pocket. "This? This is a fast-acting sedative. It just put you to sleep for a bit."

"Then why can't I fucking move?"

"That would be the Tabun. It's a nerve agent. See that patch on your hip?"

Brad lifted his head as far as he could and looked at the

patch. "What's it doing to me?" Brad asked. Desperation coated his voice.

"It's rendered your nerves useless. If I had made you inhale it, you'd be dead already, but the patch makes it release slower, delaying the effects as it absorbs into your skin." Talbot looked at his watch. "I'd say you have about twelve minutes before it paralyzes your lungs. You're probably not a medical expert, but when that happens, you won't be able to breathe."

"Please," Brad pleaded. "I can get you money. More than you could ever need!"

Talbot leaned over and picked up a large duffel bag. It was unzipped so Brad could see it was stuffed full of cash. "I already helped myself," Logan said, unable to contain his grin. "The CIA has some amazing safe-cracking tools."

"Please..."

"There is an antidote, though," Talbot said as he produced another syringe, this one full of a yellow liquid.

"Yes! Give it to me! I'll do whatever you want!"

"I'll give it to you if you do exactly what I tell you to do. But don't take too long thinking about it. Looks like you only have about nine minutes left," Talbot said casually.

"Anything, I swear! Name it!" Brad felt like he couldn't breathe. He wasn't sure if it was a panic attack or the toxin doing its thing.

"Two things, Brad. First, I want the names of your backers. You were easy to find because you're no mastermind. You're just a sniveling bitch with an internet following. The people who fund you are much better at covering their tracks, even from the CIA."

"They'll kill me!"

"You're dead in eight minutes anyway. I'd recommend

giving yourself a fighting chance."

"Okay! Okay! What's the second thing?" Brad cried.

"I'm going to go live on your channel using that camera and laptop. And you're going to tell the world everything you've done."

Logan finished the upload. His friend at the CIA had all the information Brad Dockery kept on his business partners.

Granted, it wasn't a lot. Brad was the low man on the totem pole. But it was enough to start.

Vortex had made a sniveling, tearful confession that was live-streamed to the world. He came clean about everything and told Logan how to access the files on the contestants so their families could be notified.

Logan remained off camera. He had no desire to put his identity out there. He wasn't worried about repercussions from Vortex's associates. They were going to find out he was alive and come after him no matter what. He just didn't want his face or name associated with this, even as the guy who brought Vortex down.

He closed the laptop and stuffed it in the duffel bag. As he prepared to leave, Vortex called out to him.

"Wait! What about the antidote?"

"I changed my mind."

220

"What?? I did everything you told me to!" Brad yelled in disbelief.

"So what? You did the right thing because your life was on the line. You think that makes up for a lifetime of being scum?" Logan couldn't stomach the sight of the piece of shit any longer.

"I'm sorry!"

"No, you're not. You just got caught. You learned long ago how to exploit people for your own gain. Do you think because a bunch of strangers like your videos, that somehow it gives you power over them? That you're better than them? You started out by humiliating people in your videos, and you moved on to murdering them."

"I'm sorry!" he bellowed again, choking on his last words as saliva rapidly pooled in his mouth.

"You made your confession. Now it's time to carry out your sentence."

The drool turned to foam, and the internet personality spasmed uncontrollably. He made horrid, rasping noises as he frantically searched for breath he couldn't get.

With one last intense spasm, Vortex fell still. He was dead.

Logan tossed the duffel bag over his shoulder and grabbed the decanter of obscenely expensive bourbon from the night table. He popped the lid and took a swig before pouring the rest of it over Vortex's body.

He took out Darnell Bank's lucky lighter and used it to ignite the alcohol. The booze, along with the silk sheets, went up quickly, engulfing Brad Dockery's body as the fire spread.

Logan calmly walked out the front door and down the street to his rented car as the sound of fire trucks grew in the distance.

EPILOGUE

LIVE TO PLAY
ANOTHER DAY

CHRISTMAS EVE

J ust after noon on Christmas Eve, Lieutenant Logan "LT" Talbot opened the gate affixed to a small chain-link fence. He walked up the path to the modest house. His leg, mostly healed from the gunshot, still stung, especially in the frigid December air.

He stepped onto the covered porch, which was badly in need of a paint job, and carefully set down two big boxes crudely covered in wrapping paper.

Normally he wouldn't just leave something like that in the open, but he saw the electric company van across the street and knew his agency friends would keep an eye until the occupants of the house retrieved them.

He was halfway down the path to the gate when he heard the door open. Logan turned and saw a young boy, about eight years old, standing in the doorway. The boy regarded him curiously but didn't say anything.

"You must be Liam," Logan said with a warm smile. "I'm Logan. I used to know your mom."

The boy remained silent as Logan took a step closer, moving slowly so as not to alarm him.

"Your mom wanted you to have that present."

Liam looked intrigued. He examined the box carefully, almost studying it, but he still didn't speak to him.

"Liam!" a woman's voice called from inside the house.

"What did I tell you about going outside without—"

Kasey Collins stepped into the doorway, wearing a fuzzy robe and matching slippers over her pajama bottoms and a faded Breaking Benjamin t-shirt.

She stopped in her tracks and forgot what she was saying when she saw Logan standing in front of her house. Her face registered shock before morphing to pure joy at the sight of him.

"Logan!" she said. She wanted to shout, but she was overcome with emotion, causing it to come out as more of a choked whisper.

She started toward the stairs but still had trouble walking from her many injuries. Logan rushed up the porch so she wouldn't try to move down the steps. As soon as he stepped onto the landing, she threw her arms around him and hugged tightly—as tightly as her battered body would allow. Logan returned the hug, taking care not to hurt her.

"I didn't think I'd see you again," she said as she started to cry.

"I had to handle a few things."

She pulled back and looked him over curiously. "It was you. Vortex. The confession. It was you."

He held her hands in his. "It doesn't matter."

"But-"

"Listen, Kasey," he said, getting serious and lowering his voice so Liam couldn't hear, "Vortex is dead, but the people who backed him are going to be pissed."

"What does that mean?"

"It means you need to go somewhere safe until I can take care of them."

"Take care of them? What the hell does that mean?" Kasey was getting scared, certain she knew what he meant.

"It just means you have to lie low for a bit."

"How am I supposed to do that?"

"My friends in the agency have set you up in a new location. New name. Everything." Logan had worked everything out, doing everything he could to keep them safe.

"Jesus Christ, Logan! I can't just pick up and go. What about Liam? What am I going to do for money?"

"Money won't be a problem for you ever again."

"What??" Kasey looked bewildered.

"Vortex had some lying around he wasn't going to need anymore. I sent half to my friend Alex for his treatments, and the other half is for you. My friends already opened up accounts for you under your new identity, including a college fund for Liam."

Kasey looked at him in disbelief.

"I...I just don't know what to say."

Logan squeezed her hands.

"You entered Vortex's game for a reason. Everyone did. You survived. You won. It's only fair that you get your prize. You can use that money to give your son a better life. Use it."

Her eyes filled with tears that fell down her cheeks. "What about you?"

"I kept just enough to help me finish my mission."

"Mission?"

Logan's face turned hard. "I'm going to finish healing up, then I'm going to work with the CIA on a contract basis. We're going to find every last piece of shit involved in this massacre and make them pay."

"What then?" Kasey felt a glimmer of hope in her chest.

"I'll figure it out when I'm done."

"How long until you're healed enough to leave?"

"End of next month, we figure."

She nodded, the raw emotion getting the better of her. "What about until then?"

"I'm going to lie low. Same as you."

"Come inside, then. We can lie low together." It came out as more of a plea than she wanted.

He pulled her in for another hug. "I want nothing more than that. But I can't."

She pulled away. "Why?"

"Because if I do, I'm not going to be able to leave. And this job is too important."

Kasey nodded her understanding as she bit her lip to keep from full-on sobbing.

"When I'm done, I'll find you. Maybe you'll let me buy you dinner."

She cracked a smile and sniffled. "If you really put that much money into my account, maybe I should buy you dinner."

He smiled back and kissed her on the forehead. "I'll hold you to that."

"Yes!!" Liam screamed from behind them.

They turned to face him and saw he had opened the presents to see a top-of-the-line gaming PC and monitor. He ran down the steps and hugged his mother tightly. She winced from the pain but hugged him back.

"Thank you so much, Mommy! Thank you!"

The boy was so happy he cried, which only heightened Kasey's own emotions. She gently broke the hug and, with some effort, bent down to look her son in the eye.

"My friend Logan here helped get that for you. Can you say thank you to him?"

Liam didn't hesitate to hug Logan. He was surprised,

and Kasey's look told him just how rare it was for someone else to get this reaction out of her son. He gently hugged the boy back.

"Thank you, Logan! Thank you so much!"

"You're welcome, pal. Enjoy it."

Liam turned to his mother and asked, "Can we go set it up? I know it's not Christmas 'til tomorrow but, but..."

As the boy struggled to come up with a persuasive argument, Kasey ruffled his hair. "Yes, sweetheart. Just give me a minute to say goodbye to Logan, okay?"

"Okay!" Liam agreed. He was at the apex of happiness as he bounded inside, shouting back as he scooped up his present to bring it inside. "Thanks again, Logan! Merry Christmas!"

"Merry Christmas, Liam."

He turned his focus to Kasey, her eyes telling him what her words wouldn't. *Please don't go.*

He squeezed her arm. "Merry Christmas, Kasey."

ABOUT THE AUTHOR

James Kaine picked up a copy of *The Scariest Stories You've Ever Heard* at a scholastic book fair when he was a kid and hasn't looked back since. Now an active Member of the Horror Writers Association, James, as he puts it, "lives his dream to give you nightmares." His work includes novels such as *My Pet Werewolf, Pursuit* and *The Dead Children's Playground.*

Born and raised in Trenton, NJ, James still resides in the Garden State with his wife, two children and a loveable Boston Terrier, named Obi. When not writing about horrible things, James enjoys reading, movies, music, cooking and rooting for the New York Giants. Well, maybe he doesn't enjoy that last one.

Visit www.jameskaine.com for news, merch and to join the James Kaine VIP Readers Club, netting yourself two free eBooks instantly!

f JamesKaineWrites

⊙ JamesKaineWrites

♪ @JamesKaineWrites

𝕏 JamesKaineBooks

▶ @HorrorHousePublishing

BOOKS BY JAMES KAINE

STANDALONE
Pursuit
Black Friday

MY PET WEREWOLF SERIES
My Pet Werewolf
Gunther

AMERICAN HORRORS SERIES
The Dead Children's Playground

SOME TIME LATER...

Where the hell was Chuck?

Eddie and Chuck were part of the clean-up crew working on the ruins of Oatbridge Mall. They had just dug through into the maintenance tunnel and were scouting it to determine the best way to dig it out.

They were about to head down when Eddie's lunch started talking back at him. He told Chuck to wait while he ran to the port-a-potty. It wasn't pleasant, but he made it through.

Damn enchiladas!

When he got back, Chuck was nowhere to be found. Dumb shit must have gone in ahead of him. Didn't he realize how dangerous that was?

Eddie climbed down the ladder carefully. The last thing he needed was to fall and bust his ass. If Chuck was down there and hurt, they would be fucked if Eddie ended up out of commission too.

He turned on his flashlight and made his way through a large pile of rubble. It was tight, but he made it through.

When he reached the other side, he shined his light on something that almost made him shit again, that time right in his pants.

Chuck's mangled corpse was tossed like garbage on a

pile of rocks. He was bent completely in half, and his neck was twisted all the way around, a jagged piece of spine jutting out of the top of his back. The man's last moments were etched into his terrified expression.

Eddie couldn't stop himself from screaming. His terrified cries echoed through the tunnel, drowning out the heavy footsteps of the enormous man moving toward the exit at the other end of the passage.

Printed in Great Britain
by Amazon